WOLF BLOOD

LUNAR ACADEMY, YEAR ONE

ALYSSA ROSE IVY

JENNIFER SNYDER

AXEL

*S*moke curled around my face as I exhaled. I eyed the others from where I stood near the edge of the woods, taking stock. Some drove fancy cars while others had taken the tiny town of Brentwood's public transportation system. I'd made it to town yesterday afternoon and gotten myself a room at Charity's Inn to decompress before coming to the academy.

Leaving home had been tough.

My family wasn't all rainbows and fucking sunshine, but there was still a piece of me that wanted to stay in the soul-sucking, Podunk town regardless. Leaving made me feel like I was running from what I'd done—like I was running from the memory of Ansley.

I took another puff from my cigarette. My eyes zeroed in on a tall guy with a pretty face and dark hair. He oozed confidence in a way that irked me. I watched him, taking in his swagger and the invisible chip he held on his shoulder. He was the type of guy who'd make me see red quicker than I liked. I'd have no trouble sinking my fangs into him and draining him dry simply because I was the karma I was willing to bet he had coming.

"Yo, Finn," someone called to him. Finn nodded in the guy's direction and then walked toward him. "Guys, this is Finn," I heard the guy say. "He's Ryan Grayson's second."

Neither name meant shit to me, but apparently both did to the others. Their eyes lit up. My wolf bristled as my lips curled. He was just another shmuck looking to get ahead thanks to his family name. While the guy himself might irritate me, his wolf didn't. I could sense how strong he was. Dominant. He'd piqued my wolf's interest. I tore my eyes away from him before I lost control.

Getting riled up was never good. Unless I was scheduled for a fight.

Finn seemed like someone I'd enjoy beating the shit out of for a few bucks, but with a face like that, I doubted he was the fighting type. I'd been in the underground fighting business long enough to recognize another fighter when one crossed my path.

This dude wasn't it.

I licked my lips and took another puff from my cigarette, trying to tame my wolf. He was a beast with a mind of his own. My vampire was the same. Both were a struggle for me to control. Which was why I was at Lunar Academy in the first place. Still, I couldn't help surveying the prospects for a fight. I blamed it on my wolf's insatiable need to exude dominance wherever I went, but it was just me talking shit. I liked to fight as much as my other half.

My lips twisted at the corners, forming a smirk, as something my mom used to say to me surfaced in my mind—*your fists will be the death of you.*

I scoffed. If only. My entire life, they'd been how I kept my sanity.

I took another pull from my cigarette and then glanced at the evidence of the last fight I'd been in still visible on my hands. There were a few small cuts along the knuckles of my right hand, but at least my index finger wasn't swollen all to hell anymore. Wolf Blood healing was superior to some other breeds of werewolves, thanks to our vampire side. While healing wasn't instantaneous the way a typical vampire's was, it was close. It often took about a day for me to heal up after a fight, depending on how badly I got my ass handed to me.

The guy at the bar last night had it coming though.

If I hadn't given him a beat down, someone else would've. The thought of being someone's karma floated through my head again, causing me to crack another grin. The guy had been verbally abusive to his girlfriend in front of everyone, and from the way she cowered as he shouted at her, I knew his abuse didn't stop there when they were behind closed doors. He'd deserved the busted-up face and broken ribs I'd given him.

I was sure that was why the bartender had let me get a few hits in before he tried to break us up. Most likely he'd been wanting to do the same for a while.

I lifted my boot and snuffed my cigarette out on the

bottom before flipping the butt into the woods. A wince rippled through me involuntarily. As soon as it happened, sadness crept in. Ansley had always been on me about tossing my butts like that.

Do you know how long it takes for something like that to break down?

Her words floated through my head, and I pulled in a shaky breath. I missed her. She'd been gone eight months, and yet the pain was still as raw as if it had happened yesterday.

I closed my eyes and inhaled a deep breath, trying my damnedest to not lose my shit. Now wasn't the time. It was time to check-in, and I had no intention of walking in there smelling of weakness and emotions.

The fuckers would pounce on me.

I squared my shoulders and cleared my throat. While I didn't plan to walk into the academy with an invisible chip on my shoulder like Finn had, I would be walking in with a badass vibe that screamed don't fuck with me like I did everywhere else.

The sound of a motorcycle nearing captured my attention.

"Now that's an entrance." I chuckled. If I planned on making friends with anyone while here, it would be with that guy.

I bent to pick up my duffel bag, causing the ring on my necklace—Ansley's promise ring—to slip into view. The sight triggered a ripple effect of thoughts involving her, same as always. An ache to pull out my cell and listen to the last voicemail she left built in my chest.

I chewed the inside of my cheek and ignored it.

It was for the best. If I went down that road, I'd definitely lose control, and when that happened, there was no telling who'd come out to play—my wolf or my vampire.

I squeezed the straps of my duffel bag tight, grabbed hold of Ansley's promise ring with my free hand, and kissed it. My gaze drifted to the sky. "Wish me luck, darlin'."

The rumble of the motorcycle grew louder. I stepped out of the woods and headed toward the quad where everyone was congregated. While I walked, I glanced at the bike. The driver had come to a stop behind a silver convertible filled with beautiful women wearing green tops. I didn't know much about the academy, but I was noticing a trend.

A color-coded one.

My gaze skimmed over the four girls in the convertible. Magic pulsed from them. I could smell it in the breeze. They were Wolf Bound—half werewolf, half witch—that much was clear. And, if I had to guess, I'd say green was their house color.

Eyes were on me. My wolf perked at the sensation.

I glanced around, but couldn't pinpoint where the sensation came from. However, I did notice the eyes were female the more I focused on the feeling. I kept walking. I wasn't here for flirting or hookups.

People were everywhere—talking, laughing, kissing— and the parking area was full of vehicles. I wasn't sure where the hell those waiting in line planned to park, but this space was full. I gripped my bag tighter and pulled in another deep breath, hoping to steady my inner demons. My wolf paced. He hated crowds and chaotic places. My vampire wasn't much of a fan either. All I wanted to do was check-in and figure out where my dorm room was.

The eyes I'd felt before were on me again. I didn't seek them out this time. Instead, I tried to figure out where I was supposed to go. Tables positioned in front of a building caught my eye. There were four of them. Each with a different color tablecloth.

One color for each house, I presumed.

The driver of the motorcycle grew restless and wove around the silver convertible before making their way through the crowd. As they passed, I glanced at them. It surprised me to learn the driver wasn't a dude like I'd initially thought, but a female. Her body was hugged in black leather, showcasing her curves. When she came to a stop a few feet away and pulled off her helmet, dark brown locks spilled free, reaching just past her shoulders. She straddled the bike and glanced around.

I didn't know who she was, but I knew I liked her already. Nothing screamed badass more than black leather and riding a motorcycle. Since my well-worn black leather jacket was my staple, I felt as though we were kindred spirits.

Too bad Lunar Academy forced us to wear a uniform.

My jaw ticked. That was one thing about this place I knew would piss me off. I didn't know how I'd handle being in slacks and crisp button-downs with a tie Monday through Friday. I'd never worn a tie in my life. Not even to Ansley's funeral.

My wolf nipped at me as he continued to pace. My fangs pricked my gumline. I swallowed hard, knowing I needed to calm the hell down. Wearing a uniform wouldn't be the death of me. It was no reason to go apeshit and lose control.

I wove through a group of guys, who were laughing and chatting loudly. They seemed to know one another well. I assumed they were older. Maybe second years? I picked up on the fact they were Wolf Born right away. I couldn't pinpoint how I knew; I just did.

"Excuse me," a husky female voice called. I lifted my gaze to her as if pulled by a magnet. It was the girl on the bike. "Does anyone know if we're supposed to park here, or if we can head to the garage? Is there a key card or a code I'm supposed to know before I can get in?" When no one answered her, she tossed her hands up and sighed. "Jesus, this place is going to be fun."

I cracked a grin. She was cute when she was worked up. Hell, she was cute when she wasn't, but I found something adorable about seeing her pissed.

"Hey, baby. I see you like power between them legs of yours," some asshole called to her. I chewed the inside of my cheek, watching him closer than I should. My wolf growled and tiny dots of red danced along the edges of my vision as my vampire's interest piqued too. "I've got something else you might like to ride sometime. Wanna give it a go?" He high-fived the guy beside him and laughed. It was clear he was proud of the line.

It took everything in me to stay where I was instead of marching over and decking him. Guys like him gave the rest of us a bad rep. Also, something about this girl made me want to protect her honor.

I took a step forward, but paused when she spoke.

"Since you're practically four-foot-nothing, I doubt there's enough power hanging between your legs to do much for me," she said before flipping him off.

I chuckled. I couldn't help it. It rumbled from me as I stared at the guy's reaction. She didn't wait for him to respond; instead, she revved the engine of her bike, garnering the attention of everyone close, and inched forward.

"All these spaces are full. Can we park in the garage?" she shouted to the people at her right. "Is there a key card or a code for it I need first?"

A girl wearing a yellow lanyard stepped to her and answered her question. I assumed the lanyard signified the house she was from, but I had no clue which one was yellow. It was either Wolf Born or Wolf Bitten, though.

I scanned the clusters of people near the tables in front of the building, searching for red lanyards. It had to be the color for Wolf Bloods. Blood was red, and since we were part vampire, it only made sense that we had the color for our house.

A table to my left caught my attention. There was a red tablecloth draped over it. I moved to stand in line behind a petite redhead wearing too much perfume. My wolf relaxed. We were still in a crowd and chaos surrounded us, but at least we knew what the hell we were doing now. Somewhat. The girl in front of me flipped her hair over her shoulder, sending a whiff of her perfume to my nose. It coated the inside of my mouth and made me cough.

Didn't she realize a little went a long way with perfume and a werewolf's sense of smell? The potent amount she wore could easily be considered guy repellent. Seriously. I coughed in my hand again, and she turned around to flash me the nastiest look I'd been given in a while.

The girl on the bike revved her engine once more, drawing my attention back to her, as she inched forward again. When she eased past me, our eyes locked. Her plump red lips twisted into a smirk, and I knew right then and there I was in trouble.

If I wasn't careful, this girl would derail me.

I tore my eyes from hers and focused on the slow-moving line in front of me. Her eyes remained on me. I could feel them, but I didn't glance at her again. I couldn't. I'd made a promise. And, I wouldn't let her sidetrack me from it.

FAITH

*H*e was sexy as all get-out, but he wasn't my type. Not anymore. Not with this new version of me. I'd only smirked at him, because I could see forced rejection in his eyes directed my way. It wasn't anything I hadn't seen before. There were plenty of men at the bar I'd worked at back home who looked my way with it festering in their eyes. Mainly because they were married or in committed relationships and trying not to lead me on or start something up. I was fine with that type of rejection—in fact; I applauded it. It took a real man to love a woman so hard he refused himself any others—but that wasn't the forced rejection Mr. Leather Jacket had given me.

His stemmed from a place of fear.

I knew I appeared intimidating to some; I'd learned that about myself at a young age, but I also knew that wasn't this guy's problem either. Whoever he was, he wasn't rejecting me because of that. He was rejecting me because he was broken.

A woman he loved had either done him dirty or died.

I knew the look well. It was the same one Van had worn often back home. I'd ignored it then, but I refused to ever ignore it in a man again. It had kept him forever at arm's length in our relationship, and I knew I deserved better.

It might have taken me awhile to see it, but now that I did, there was no going back to being that naive girl. Loving someone still in love with the memory of someone else wasn't worth my time. Four long months, and too many tears, was how long it had taken me to realize that.

I exhaled a breath, relaxing my features and maneuvered my bike around a group of girls who didn't seem to care they were blocking traffic. They were too caught up in talking about their perfect summer and hugging.

I fought the urge to glance back at Mr. Leather Jacket as I crept along at a snail's pace.

I wasn't here to date. I wasn't here for hookups either. I was here for a fresh start. A new beginning. One that didn't involve my mom and her wacky traditional vampire ways. One that had nothing to do with those from the nest she'd been a part of since I was born. They were all too cultlike for my taste. I had never fit in, and I knew that I never would because I was part werewolf. I'd accepted this a long time ago, but that didn't mean I liked it.

This place... it would be different.

I would fit in because I wasn't the only hybrid. I

wasn't an outcast or an oddball because of it. I was just another student here to learn among my peers.

Still, it didn't hurt to look at some eye candy while I was here, right? I glanced over my shoulder at Mr. Leather Jacket when I came to a full stop thanks to a bunch of guys not giving a shit I was in motion. He was in line at a table, staring into the distance. The car behind me beeped, and I jerked back around to head into the garage Darcie—the girl with the yellow lanyard nice enough to help—had mentioned. She'd told me to go around the back of the building and look for the door tucked between the two tallest hedges.

I was trying, but people were idiots.

When I finally made it inside the garage, I slipped off my bike and popped open the storage compartment to grab my bag. I'd only brought my favorite articles of clothing with me and a few other essentials. A tinge of sadness pinched at my insides from the way I'd left in the night, but it was for the best. Besides, starting fresh meant getting new stuff. And getting new stuff was always fun. I couldn't wait to check out the shops in Brentwood. I'd cashed out a large sum from my bank account to get me by for a while, but I'd feel more content if I snagged a job somewhere. I had noticed a bar called Last Call when I came through town. Maybe they'd be hiring bartenders since I was sure the academy being in session upped their customer base each night. I'd heard the place didn't have the usual twenty-one and over rule for drinking that typical places had. Apparently, the owner was in on an academy for werewolves being nearby. Maybe he was one. I wasn't sure. Either way, I was hoping to snag a job there. Bartending was something I enjoyed. Smith, from my mom's nest back home, had got me a fake ID two summers ago that said I was twenty-one. That was how I'd been able to bartend at sixteen. I'd thanked him a million times for giving me that ID.

Damn, I would miss him.

I slung my bag over my shoulder and placed my helmet inside the compartment on my bike before locking it. As I pocketed my keys, my gaze darted around at the well-lit garage hidden beneath the academy. It was massive. Heck, the academy was larger than I'd imagined. My wolf paced at the surge of anxiety pulsing through me. I ignored her and bit my bottom lip as I started walking back the way I'd come. The silver convertible I'd been behind before zoomed into the garage and parked in a row marked for upperclassman. The driver—a busty blonde with perfect features—gave me a nasty look as she cut the engine of her car. The others in her squad followed suit.

"Wolf Bloods are so predictable. Hotheaded and impatient. I seriously don't understand why the academy allows them to attend school here with the rest of us," she said to her groupies, loud enough for me to hear. They nodded in agreement and flashed me a nasty look that mirrored hers.

I rolled my eyes. Her and her sheep didn't faze me. I'd dealt with mean girls before. They weren't worth my time.

I continued outside and made my way around to the

front of the building again. Once there, I became lost in the crowd trying to make my way to the table for Wolf Blood's house. An older guy—who I presumed to be a teacher—motioned for me to veer right.

"Wolf Blood information is that way," he said before shifting his attention to the next student behind me.

I gave him a thumbs up and continued walking. Mr. Leather Jacket was no longer in line, or at least I couldn't see him from where I was. A part of me was disappointed. However, deep down I knew it was probably for the best.

He was a distraction I didn't need.

My gaze drifted to the center building. It looked like a castle. There wasn't much I knew about Lunar Academy other than it had been here for ages, which meant the possibility of it being an actual castle was strong.

"Honey, you only wish you were Wolf Bound," a familiar bitchy voice said from nearby. I glanced in her direction. If she was talking to me, I planned on telling her where she could go with her attitude. When I spotted her, her attention was on a brown-haired mousy-looking girl with more suitcases than she could carry. "Your house line is right over there. Step behind Biker Chick."

I folded my arms over my chest and glared at her. Biker Chick? Eh, I'd been called worse before.

"Oh, okay," the mousy brunette said as she struggled to gather her suitcases. It was painful to watch. Not because she wasn't strong enough to carry them—being in the Wolf Blood house meant she was part vampire and had physical strength because of it—but because two of the suitcases she was manhandling were nearly taller than her. She was a tiny thing. While I wasn't an Amazon woman, I had a few inches on her. "I didn't realize I was in the wrong line, so thanks for pointing it out." Her cheeks puffed out as she exhaled forcefully, and I knew, like me, she had to be a first year.

I left my place in line to help her with her suitcases. "I see Barbie is giving you problems too." I nodded in the busty blonde's direction. Her attention had dipped to a group of guys standing at a nearby table. "She's such a peach, isn't she?"

"Yeah, a rotten one." The pint-sized brunette smirked.

I liked her already.

We stepped back into line for the Wolf Blood table, hauling her gigantic suitcases with us, and I introduced myself to her properly. "I'm Faith, by the way, but you're free to call me Biker Chick. I'm sure there will be others who do thanks to Barbie."

"I've never been one for nicknames, so I'll stick with Faith. I'm Nora." She hoisted her backpack higher on her shoulder and then nodded to her three suitcases. "Thanks for helping. I'm not a light packer."

"I noticed." I chuckled. I wiggled the suitcase in front of me. The thing was heavy. "What's in this one? Bricks?"

"Something like that." She grinned. "So, are you a first year too?"

"Yeah. We can brave this craziness together."

Her brows pinched together as she gave me a once-over. "Seriously? I figured you were an upperclassman because you only have a backpack. You must be a light packer!"

"Not really. There just wasn't much I wanted to bring with me. I plan on heading into town for stuff once I settle in." I shrugged.

The line moved forward, and I dragged Nora's gigantic suitcase behind me as we stepped forward. A stern-faced older man I assumed was a teacher caught my eye. He stood behind the upperclassman sitting in chairs with stacks of papers in front of them and markers in hand. My eyes remained glued to the man. Not because he was hot—which he was, for an older guy—but because of his muscles.

He was seriously ripped and kind of scary.

I didn't know what he taught, but I hoped I didn't get him as a teacher. Whatever subject was bound to be as intense as he seemed, and I wasn't sure I could handle it.

"So, do you know anyone else here? Like do you have any siblings that go here?" Nora asked, still trying to keep our small talk going. "Cousins? Family friends' kids? I feel like everyone here already knows each other."

I glanced around. "It seems that way, doesn't it?" My gaze shifted back to her. "This place is cliquish. Then again, what else would you expect when we're split into groups upon entry?"

She wrinkled her nose. "Just makes it feel too cliquish."

"I know what you mean."

"I hear the uniforms are color-coded too," a guy standing in line behind us chimed in. He had jet black hair and dark eyes that looked soulful. His shirt was for a band I liked, but I didn't comment on it.

Not here for guys, I told myself as I turned back around, ignoring him.

"Red isn't my color," Nora muttered to the guy.

"Mine either, but I guess that's something we'll all have to get used to," the guy said with a chuckle. I didn't look back at him.

"To answer your earlier question—no siblings, cousins, or family friends' kids," I said, steering the conversation back to the two of us. "I don't know anyone here." Excitement pulsed through me at admitting such a simple thing. I'd always been a part of my mother's nest, but now I was on my own.

It felt good. It felt right.

"I'm on my own here too. Not that I'm an only child —I'm actually the middle kid of three—but I am the only one here. Well, for now anyway."

"What's that mean?" The line moved forward again, and I pulled her giant suitcase along with me as I walked.

"My older brother was supposed to come last year, but he decided the academy experience wasn't for him. Honestly, I'm glad because it's not like our family would've been able to send us both. Heck, they couldn't even pay for all my tuition. And, my little sister is still little. She's ten, so the academy isn't even a thought yet."

I nodded. "Got ya."

It was clear that just because Nora looked shy and

mousy, it didn't mean that she was. The girl was definitely a talker. I'd hate to see what she was like caffeinated first thing in the morning.

"What about you?" She glanced at me. "Are you on a scholarship, or are you paid tuition?"

The way she said paid tuition felt a bit judgy. It made me not want to answer. Having money had never been an issue for my family since the nest was a collective. Everyone pooled their resources, which included money, houses, and cars.

"Um, paid tuition," I muttered, uncomfortable.

Nora's brows shot up. "Oh. Sorry for the way that sounded. I didn't mean to judge or sound like I was." She swiped a stray strand of hair from her eyes as a breeze blew. "Geez, talk about a foot-in-mouth moment."

I flashed her a smile. "It's okay. Don't worry about it."

The line moved again, positioning us as next.

"Name?" a young guy sitting at the table asked without looking at me. His gaze was fixed on the stack of papers in front of him, his black marker poised and ready to cross my name out.

"Faith Brooks." It felt strange to not use my real last name of Clairemont, but changing to Brooks was part of leaving my past behind.

It was added protection to insure it.

The guy flipped a few pages into his stack. When he found my name, he marked it out and then handed me a stapled packet of papers. "This is everything you should need. The welcome speech starts in about ten minutes in the great hall, which is in the building behind me. You'll meet your advisor there. You'll be given more information there too."

"Thanks." I took the packet and then stepped to the side, taking Nora's luggage with me.

I glanced at the first paper. It was a standard welcome letter. Next was a map of the campus. It didn't seem too big, which was nice. I noticed the first-year dorms were on the fourth floor of each dormitory building. That had pros and cons. I wouldn't have to hear people above me, but the fourth floor was a long way from being on ground level. And... there didn't seem to be any elevators.

At least not on my map.

I glanced at the stone building in front of me again. What did I expect when the place looked like a castle? Elevators were too modern for this place. Still, I hoped they at least had a decent Wi-Fi connection.

"Okay, got my packet too," Nora said. She moved to stand beside me and glanced at her packet. "Anything good in here?"

"Seems basic." I shrugged as I flipped to the last page. Rules. I read them silently and then rolled my eyes. "Did you get to the rules yet?"

"What page is that?"

"The last one."

Nora flipped through her packet. She scoffed as she read, and I skimmed them again.

1. *No shifting except during school sanctioned times.*

2. *No leaving campus in wolf form.*
3. *No feeding from others.*
4. *No use of magic against others.*
5. *No use of magic outside of select classrooms.*
6. *No fighting.*
7. *No parties.*

"How MANY DO you think will be broken this year?" Nora asked with a grin.

I waved her words away. "Oh, please. How many do you think will be broken by the end of the week?"

"You're probably right." She laughed and then started lugging her suitcases toward the great hall.

It was time to meet our advisors, figure out our roommate situation, and get settled in. I couldn't wait. As I walked beside Nora, still hauling one of her gigantic suitcases behind me, I glanced at the others making their way into the building. They were an eclectic group. Some of them had me thinking a few of the school rules might end up being broken tonight from the way they looked.

Yeah, this place would definitely be interesting.

AXEL

*M*y back pressed against the wall as I surveyed those crowding into the great hall, waiting for the welcome speech to start. I wasn't sure how long this would take, but I hoped it was quick. My wolf couldn't handle being in a crowd of this size for long. He was already gnashing his teeth and growling whenever someone got too close. My vampire was barely hanging on too. His fangs were ready to prick through my gumline and sink into someone.

I needed to get out of here and decompress soon. If not, I was at risk of breaking more than a few of their rules.

My lungs filled with a deep breath to calm my inner demons, but it didn't help. The large room was growing smaller by the second as more crammed through the double doors. The air was stuffy and thick. I slipped my leather jacket off and draped it over my arm.

Didn't they have air-conditioning in this place? I

fanned my t-shirt and exhaled a puff of air. It was like an oven in here.

"And, he's got tattoos," the dark-haired girl standing beside me muttered to her friend. She had to know I could hear her. Hell, she had to know I'd felt her, and her friend's, eyes on me since they stepped into the damn room and found a spot to stand beside me. "Why do tattoos always make guys ten times hotter?"

"Because it proves they're bad boys," the other girl said with a giggle.

I didn't look at either of them. I didn't speak. I wasn't in the mood.

Instead, I put more distance between myself and them. This had me stepping closer to the upperclassman wearing red lanyards. I assumed one of them would most likely be my advisor.

More people crowded into the room. We had to be over max occupancy by now, but no one seemed to care. I did though. My wolf felt claustrophobic as hell, and my vampire was starved, which had me feeling crabby and in desperate need of a cigarette.

I glanced at the front of the room, searching for whoever was in charge of this shit show. It didn't take me but two seconds to pinpoint the headmaster of Lunar Academy. He stood among the other teachers looking prim and proper. His eyes scanned those of us crammed into the room, waiting for him to speak. What was he waiting for—silence? If so, I was down to yell at everyone to shut the fuck up.

Someone bumped me from the side and my wolf

almost snapped; his irritation had reached a new high. A snarl slipped past my lips as I glanced to see who it was. My wolf was too close to the surface.

Ice water crashed through my veins the instant I realized who'd bumped me—the girl with the motorcycle.

"Chill." Her eyes flashed with irritation that matched my own before it simmered out. "This freaking thing is huge—I'm pretty sure Nora packed her whole house—and they've got us crammed in here like sardines. I didn't bump you on purpose." A sarcastic smirk, which did things to me it shouldn't, twisted at her red lips.

I didn't know who Nora was, but if she looked anything like this girl, then I needed to keep my distance.

"I might have," a petite brunette said as she maneuvered two large suitcases and a bag to where we stood. "You never know what you might need."

"Anyway," the girl with the motorcycle said. She shifted her attention from her friend back to me. When our eyes locked this time, my wolf had calmed down enough for me to notice the finer details about her, like her hazel eyes. One seemed a little greener than the other, but it could be the shitty lighting in this place. "I'm Faith, and I'm a Wolf Blood... which I'm guessing you are too."

Faith? It always struck me as odd when people named their kids after things like that. I'd once met a little girl named Miracle. All I could think about every time her parents said her name was, why the hell did they need to name her that? Couldn't they see the miracle she represented by looking at her daily? It seemed redundant to me to make it her name.

Faith was one of those redundant names. You either had faith or you didn't. There was no reason to name your kid after it.

"I am." My voice sounded harsh, but it was probably for the best. I didn't want her to think I was flirting with her, or even the slightest bit interested, because I was talking to her. Some chicks were crazy like that. Although, I knew some guys could be too. Crazy didn't discriminate. "I'm Axel." I almost didn't give her my name. Not doing so would've made me seem like a complete ass though.

"Hey, I'm Nora," the petite brunette said as she glanced around Faith and flashed me a smile.

"Hi," I said before Faith drew my attention to her as she peeled out of her leather jacket. It hadn't gotten any cooler in here.

"I see you're not wearing a lanyard," she said. "Must be a first year like us, then."

My gaze dipped to the white crop top she wore. It hugged her chest perfectly, accentuating the fact that she wasn't wearing a bra. One could argue that because she was braless and drove a motorcycle she craved attention in the worst way, but my gut told me that couldn't be further from the truth.

Faith didn't crave attention from anyone; she just didn't give a fuck what people thought of her. At least that was my impression.

"Yeah," I muttered in response to her comment about being a first year.

I folded my arms over my chest and looked straight ahead. It was all to make myself look intimidating, but it didn't seem to work on Faith. Nora was a different story. She shifted on her feet as though the hard set to my jaw and my stance had made her uneasy. Not Faith. She continued to stare at me as though trying to pick me apart. I licked my lips and glanced at her after a beat.

"Well, I'm sure we'll see each other around, then." Her hazel eyes flashed before she shifted her attention back to Nora.

I should have looked away from her, but I couldn't. Was she playing hard to get? Was that why she seemed so nonchalant with me?

Did it matter?

Fuck no. I wasn't here to date. I was here to learn control. It was a promise I'd made.

"May I have everyone's attention," the guy on stage I'd pegged earlier as the headmaster said. His voice was deep. Commanding. The chatter in the room died down as everyone shifted their attention to him. "Thank you. I'd like to welcome you to Lunar Academy. We're glad to have the upperclassman back for another year, and just as eager to welcome those new to the academy as well. You should have all received a packet upon check-in. In it, you should find our welcome letter, a map of the campus, and also our rules. You know how this goes. All of you. This isn't the first time you've ever been read a list of rules on the first day of school. Please abide by the rules listed. They benefit us all."

There were some murmurs of annoyance from a few around me, but it was to be expected.

"Moving on... if I could have the advisors raise their hands, please. Upperclassman, you may make your way to your advisor from last year, who will have the name of your new advisor. If you're a first year, please make your way to someone holding a flag with your house color. They will direct you to your advisor, who will then pair you with a roommate and lead you to your dorm house where you will find your room. They will also have your schedule. First years are on the fourth floor of the dormitory buildings. Please remember, there are no elevators. These buildings are old, and even with the help of magic, we could only do so much." He cracked a grin, but no one else seemed to find the no elevator bit as comical as he did. "I look forward to getting to know all of you, and to another fantastic year here at Lunar Academy. Thank you."

The room exploded in chaos as everyone found their way to an advisor. My wolf bristled when somebody bumped into me, and my vampire became more irritated by the second. I popped my knuckles as I inched forward, not because I was looking for a fight, but because I needed to do something with my hands.

"There's an advisor with a red flag," Nora said as she steered her two gigantic suitcases toward a pissed off-looking dude. "I don't know if these dorm rooms are coed or what, but he should be able to help us get steered in the right direction if not."

"I imagine we're supposed to have a female advisor," Faith said. She followed behind Nora toward the guy, anyway.

The wheel to one of Nora's suitcases snapped off and rolled away. She either didn't notice or didn't care. Until it made a screeching noise as it scraped against the floor behind her.

I tried not to laugh.

"Here, let me help." I hoisted the suitcase up with one hand. The sucker was heavier than I thought it would be. Faith had been right in thinking Nora had packed her whole damn house.

"Oh." Nora blinked. "Thanks."

"No problem."

I could feel eyes on me—Faith's eyes. When I glanced at her, there was a shit-eating grin twisting the corners of her lips.

"I've got you pegged, Axel," she insisted. Her eyes narrowed, but her grin never wavered.

No one ever had me pegged. I'd been told my whole life I wasn't an easy person to read. It was often something I prided myself on. There was no way she'd done so in the handful of words we'd said to one another. "Is that so?"

"Absolutely. You're a bad boy with a soft center. All of this—" She gestured to the length of me, focusing on my tattoos and muscles. "—is a front." Confidence oozed from her.

It irked me she thought she knew me so well.

"You know nothing about me," I snarled.

"Maybe not, but I think I'm picking up on who you are." The green in her eyes flashed brighter.

A crooked grin pulled at my mouth. "Why? Because I offered to help someone carry a suitcase with a broken wheel? That tells you so much about me, doesn't it?" I was being defensive as hell and a complete asshole, but I didn't care.

This was how I kept people at arm's length.

I tore my eyes away from Faith and stepped around Nora to the guy we'd all been walking toward with the red flag. My jaw was tight. My shoulders were tense. And both my demons were wondering what the fuck had just happened. How had this girl I'd met two seconds ago gotten under my skin so bad?

"All right, my name is Pete, and these are the guys on my list," the guy with the red flag said, his gaze dipped to a stack of papers in his hand. He lowered his other arm and crammed the red flag in his back pocket. I listened as he read through his list of names. Lucky mine was at the end. "If I said your name, then you're where you need to be. If I didn't, then you're not. Move on to the next advisor."

He cut right to the point and didn't waste any time. I liked that. It was something I could respect.

"Oh! We're over there!" Nora shouted. "I heard her say both of our names." She nodded to the blonde standing a few feet away. She took her suitcase from me and stacked it onto the one with all its wheels, muttered thank you, and then headed in that direction.

Faith should have followed her, but instead, she stared at me. Was she waiting for me to speak? To apologize maybe?

She shouldn't hold her breath.

I cut my gaze from her to Pete, my advisor, and gripped the handle of my duffle bag tight. Eventually, she got the memo I had nothing else to say to her and started after Nora. Something inside me relaxed at the distance between us, and I could focus on what Pete was staying.

"All right, let's make this short and sweet. Obviously, you're in Wolf Blood. I'll take you to our dorm house, and then pair you with your roommate once we're there. Sound good?" He didn't wait for anyone to answer. Instead, he started toward the double doors. "Okay, good. Grab your shit and let's get walking. Like the headmaster said, there are no elevators. You'll get used to it. You have no choice."

I followed behind him, ready to get out of this oven they called the great hall and into some fresh air.

Dark clouds had rolled in while I'd been inside, signaling rain would come at some point. There was a cool breeze as I walked with the others toward the Wolf Blood dormitory, but it felt good against my clammy skin. I lit the cigarette I'd been craving, not caring if it was allowed. No one said anything to me as I walked. Not even Pete. My gaze drifted to my roommate prospects while my boots thudded against the walkway between the buildings. Out of them all, there wasn't one I cared to be tied to for the year. My wolf tried to feel them each out, but there was no point. He was too ramped up from everything today to focus.

Pete paused in front of a building that looked like all the others—stone, intimidating, and large. He placed his back to it as he spun to face us and grinned. "And here it is, boys. Home, sweet home. There are only a few rules— keep your space clean, keep your noise level down, no girls are allowed in the rooms past midnight, and always remember that Wolf Bloods rule." He stepped to the door and swung it open before heading inside.

Everyone followed behind him, but I hung back. I didn't want to be crammed into another crowd as I made my way up however many flights of stairs to the fourth floor. Also, I needed one more drag off my cigarette. I snuffed it out on the bottom of my boot, and tucked the butt in my front pocket before heading inside.

"Here's the main lounge," Pete said as he gestured to the area we'd walked into.

Red couches were spread throughout the area. There was a large TV on one of the walls and some wall art hung around the area. In the back section, there was a pool table, a couple of dartboards, and a few tables I imagined were often used for playing cards. Overall, it was more sophisticated than I had anticipated. I could imagine myself relaxing here on a Friday night.

"You'll notice a lot of things are red because, as you all know, red is our color." Pete nodded to another room on the opposite side of the staircase he was leading us to. "In there are a couple vending machines where you can grab a late-night snack, a bag of blood for a pick me up, or a rushed morning breakfast if you're late for class."

My stomach grumbled at the mention of blood. My vampire was famished.

"Fourth years are on the first floor, third years on the second floor, second years on the third floor, and first years are on the fourth floor. I have no idea why it's done that way, but it is. Like the headmaster said, there are no elevators. Like I said previously, you'll get used to it, so don't start bitching." Pete started up at the wide staircase and motioned for us to follow. "On each floor are dorms for us and the ladies, communal bathrooms, and a small shared lounge." His pace on the stairs picked up. As did everyone else's.

When we finally reached the fourth floor, Pete paired people up. I waited for my name to be called.

"Stone and Twain." He held out two papers, which I assumed were schedules. A nerdy guy stepped forward. My roommate. He glanced at both papers before taking the one meant for him. I took mine next. "Last are Wilson and Yates. Rooms are marked by your last names. Make sure you check-in with Professor Sinclaire in the main lounge and get your ID made. Your rooms are unlocked as of now, but locks will engage at six tonight. If you don't have your ID, you can't get in. IDs are also used in the dining hall and all vending machines. Don't lose them. Have fun getting settled in, boys." He was gone before anyone could ask questions.

If I ever became an advisor, that was exactly how I'd be.

My skin prickled as a set of eyes scanned me. Twain's eyes.

"What?" I snapped, glancing at him.

"Nothing. I just can't believe you're who they paired me with."

I arched a brow. "Got a problem with it?"

"Nope. Not at all." His face blanched. "It's an odd combination is all. You'd think they'd put us with people we might have things in common with to keep levels of hostility down."

Even though he had a point, I didn't say so.

The guy was nerdy as hell. My demons didn't see a need to be hostile toward him. Maybe they had paired us right after all.

FAITH

My room wasn't anything impressive, but then again, I hadn't expected it to be. I would have been fine with anything, honestly. There were two beds—both twins—positioned on opposite sides of the room, a window above each, a desk along the far wall sat between them with storage space above it, two tiny dressers on opposite sides of the room, and one closet.

"Wow, this place is huge!" Nora insisted.

She pulled the two oversized suitcases she'd been lugging around into the room behind her. I'd swapped her out for the one with the missing wheel on the stairs. I leaned it against the wall and then spun to face her.

"It's decent," I said.

"I'm used to sharing a room much smaller than this with my sister." Her eyes widened as she tossed her backpack on the bed to the right of the door. "Look at that bookshelf above the desk!"

It was odd to see someone get so excited over storage space, but who was I to judge? We all had our thing.

I closed the dorm door and locked it. Nora gave me a look.

"What? Safety is important." I slung my backpack on the bed to the left of the door.

"I guess." She placed her hands on her hips and walked around to survey the room. "Are you set on that bed?"

"Yeah, I am." I unzipped my backpack and pulled out its contents. "I sleep on my left side and would rather not sleep on a bed where my face has to be squished against a cold wall while doing so."

It was a lie. I didn't give a crap if my face touched the wall. I just preferred having a wall to my back then a door anyone could barge into. I didn't like people sneaking up behind me. Especially not while I was sleeping.

"Okay. Just checking." She unzipped the suitcase on her bed. "We should probably split everything down the middle. We can share the top of the desk but maybe alternate drawers and halve the shelves above it. It looks like we get our own dressers, which is good, but we have to share a closet."

I stuffed the clothes I'd brought into the dresser. When I was done, I set my toiletries bag on the dresser and put my backpack on the floor beside it. Then, I grabbed the bag of blood I'd brought with me. I was famished. After I popped a straw in it, I kicked off my boots and lay across my new bed. It was surprisingly comfortable. Part of me had thought it would be lumpy.

When I glanced at Nora, I noticed she was busy pulling a million things out of her suitcase. None of which were clothes or toiletries. The chick had an entire suitcase of paperbacks.

Apparently, I was rooming with a bookworm.

"You know, they make these things called e-books now. They also have special devices called e-readers and certain companies have apps you can download on your phone, so you don't have to lug around a suitcase of books like that," I teased.

At first, I didn't think she heard me. She seemed too busy inspecting the edges of her books as she pulled them from the suitcase, but then, she glanced over her shoulder at me.

"I have an e-reader and an app on my phone. These are just my favorites." She smiled. "Some of them are signed editions. They're priceless."

When she didn't laugh, I knew she was serious.

I blinked as I took an extra-long pull off my straw. Satisfying blood coated the inside of my mouth, and I swallowed hard as I continued to stare at Nora. I'd never met someone so serious about books before. While I enjoyed reading here and there, I wouldn't describe myself as a reader.

Nora was different.

She handled her books with care. I heard her sigh when she pulled them from the suitcase and watched as she caressed their covers.

Books were clearly her life, and I loved that.

"If you had to pick one book or series out of all of

those as your favorite, which would you choose?" I asked, finding myself more curious than I cared to admit.

"Don't ask me to pick because I can't." She cast me a sideways glance. "Which is why I brought an entire suitcase of books with me. I couldn't leave them behind. My sister would've destroyed them somehow. She isn't much of a reader. And when she is, she bends the book in ways you shouldn't and dog ears the corners. It drives me insane!"

"Have you always loved to read?"

"Oh, yeah. As soon as I learned how, I became addicted. They're an escape from reality. You can go anywhere and be anything between their pages." She flashed me a nervous smile. "I know that sounds stupid."

I shook my head. "Not at all." It didn't sound stupid; it sounded amazing. I didn't know what it felt like to be so passionate about something. Well, maybe Stella. My bike was my freedom. My escape. Exactly like Nora's books were for her. "You can have all the shelves above the desk for them if you want."

Her eyes widened. "Are you serious?"

"Yeah. I don't have anything to put there, and all my textbooks will probably stay in my backpack."

"Awesome, thanks! And, you can borrow any of them you want. Just be careful not to screw up the cover or bend the pages. Use a bookmark." She grabbed a stack of five books and set them on the top shelf above the desk with so much care it was almost comical.

"If one grabs my attention, I will. But I'm not really a reader," I admitted.

She flashed me a look that let me know right away those could be fighting words if this conversation continued. I flashed her a coy smile.

"I just don't get that. How can you say you're not a reader? I don't understand when people aren't into books." She stared at me, waiting for me to explain.

I sipped my bag of blood, not knowing what to say. I didn't have a particular reason. I just wasn't into reading. "I've never allowed myself to get lost in much of anything." I shrugged, but it was the truth, and I was surprised it had come to me so easily.

A touch of sadness dimmed her eyes. She turned to grab another stack of books and moved to set them on the shelf beside the others. "Why?"

I'd known the question was coming, because I'd set myself up for it. "I don't know."

It was an honest answer. It was also the only one she would get from me on the subject.

"There has to be something you allow yourself to get lost in," Nora said. Her words were soft. She wasn't prying for the sake of prying; she was genuinely attempting to get to know me.

"Guys. Work. Riding my bike." My answers seemed typical. Boring. Well, all except for the mention of my bike.

"Oh, well. I guess that works too. Escaping into guys isn't a terrible thing." Her lips curled upward at the corners, and I questioned whether her whole librarian act was a front. Did Nora have a wild side? "Speaking of guys, it seemed like you and Axel—wasn't that his name?—have chemistry." She wiggled her eyebrows.

I finished the rest of my bag of blood before tossing it in the tiny trash can underneath the desk. "Even if we did, I wouldn't try to pursue it."

"Why not? He's gorgeous. Don't tell me he's not your type."

I slipped off my bed and crossed the room to browse the titles she still had to shelve. "Oh, he's definitely my type."

"Then what's the problem?"

"I'm not here to date." My tone was far more serious than was necessary, but my words had been more of a reminder to myself than an answer to her question.

Axel was just as broken as I was—if not more—and two broken people didn't make someone whole.

"What? This place is the equivalent of human college. That's all people do is date." Nora grabbed the stack of books in front of me and moved to put them on the shelf with the others.

"Yeah, well, I've always done things against the grain. My experience at the academy won't be any different. I'm here to focus on more important things than guys and partying." I clamped my lips together. If I said anything else, I might open myself up to more questions.

"Partying is against the rules, remember?" She smirked.

Oh, this girl was going to be fun, and I knew we would be the best of friends.

The issue I saw us running into was that Nora was

easy to talk to, which meant it would be difficult to keep my secret from her.

"What kind of things are you hoping to focus on?" Her question was tentative. It was clear she wasn't sure she should ask, but had pressed forward anyway.

"Things I'd rather not talk about." I grabbed a stack of books with blue spines. They seemed to be in the same series, but I could be wrong. "Want me to help you put these up? Or I can unpack another suitcase for you?"

I wanted the topic of conversation to change, but didn't want to seem rude.

"Yeah, sure. You can put the rest of these up there, thanks." She stepped to another suitcase. I noticed then the one with all the books was the one missing the wheel. No wonder. That sucker was heavy. "Oh, and I have an extra blanket and set of sheets if you want to borrow them until you head into town for something else. The stuff here doesn't seem comfortable. I'm glad I brought my own."

My fingers smoothed along the blanket on Nora's bed. The fabric was scratchy, but the sheets were the worst. "Great, thanks. I'll have to make a trip to town soon and grab something else. These academy-issued ones do suck."

She passed me the sheets and extra blanket. "No problem."

I tossed them on my bed and then directed my attention back to the books in front of me.

Once all of Nora's stuff was unpacked, she pulled out

a box of Cheez-It crackers from her snack supplies and held them out to me.

"Want some? I have a Netflix subscription. We can find a movie and watch it on my laptop while snacking." Her eyes brightened. Clearly, this was something she did often.

"Actually, we should probably get our IDs. Then, I was thinking about heading to the dining hall. Maybe finding something a little less juvenile than your current snack choice to eat." I'd already sustained my vampire, but now my wolf wanted something protein-packed.

"Let me know what their options are. Maybe check out the vending machines downstairs too." She propped her head up with her pillow and opened the box of crackers. The cheddar aroma filled the air, making my stomach growl. "I'll seek out the professor doing the IDs in a bit."

"Um, no. You're coming with me. It's the first night. You can't sit here by yourself, eating crackers and watching a movie on your laptop," I insisted.

"Why not?" She popped a few in her mouth. "It's been a long day. I doubt anyone will be in the dining hall. They're probably still unpacking." She set her laptop on her lap and pushed the button to boot it up.

I grabbed it from her and put it on the desk. Next, I took her box of crackers. "Doubtful. They're probably in the lounge area of their houses, walking around campus, or in the dining hall figuring out who they want to screw and where the big back-to-school party will be."

"I don't know," Nora whined.

"Yeah, well, I do. Get up. Let's get our IDs made, and

then head to the dining hall so we at least know where to go to for breakfast in the morning." I knew if I tossed in a practical reason she'd be all for it. Nora reminded me of the only female friend I'd had while growing up, Tasha.

My cell chimed with a new text, startling me.

A sick feeling twisted in the pit of my stomach because no one had my new number. No one except Tasha. If she was texting me, it wasn't going to be about anything good.

My cell chimed for a second time, reminding me I hadn't glanced at the text yet.

"Aren't you going to see who that is?" Nora asked. The area between her brows wrinkled as they pinched together in concern. "Why do you look like you're about to throw up?"

I forced a smile onto my face. "I'm fine."

My fingers shook as I pulled my cell from my back pocket and glanced at the screen.

What did you do?

The words sent dread flooding through my system. My throat pinched tight. Tasha had given my number out, and even though this number wasn't one I had saved in my phone, I knew it well.

It was Van's.

He hadn't gotten my number from Tasha because he missed me. He hadn't gotten it because he wanted to check on me either. He'd gotten it because they'd found Xavier's body, and he knew he was dead because of me.

AXEL

I put out my cigarette before following Lee into the dining hall. Being in a crowded area among students and faculty again wasn't where I wanted to be. I would rather be in our dorm, screwing around on my phone alone, but he'd said he would buy me something to eat, and I never turned down a free meal.

So, here I was.

I wasn't sure why he'd wanted to come here in the first place, but he'd seemed adamant. Part of me thought maybe it was because he saw some chick he was interested in earlier, but then I remembered how minutes before we left our dorm to get our IDs made he'd been alphabetizing his comic book collection, and I knew that couldn't be the case.

Any guy who was that into comic books had no fucking clue how to talk to women.

And, comic books were his life. Not only did he have a slew of them, but he also collected comic book cards.

There was one specific card he'd shown me at least ten times since he'd unpacked. It was signed by the creator of the character and kept in a plastic display case. He'd put it in our shared closet on the center shelf so every time he opened the doors he saw it.

He might be a total nerd, but I could tell he would grow on me. My wolf and vampire seemed to like him too, which counted for a lot since both of them were even bigger assholes than me.

I'd been worried my wolf would want to exude dominance over him since we were staying in such tight quarters together, or that my vampire might want to fight him, but neither seemed to find him a threat or challenge.

To say I was relieved was an understatement.

"This place isn't bad," Lee said as we stepped farther into the dining hall. "There are more people here than I thought there would be, though. I guess everyone had the idea to grab something to eat." He flashed me a nervous smile.

"Yeah, looks like."

I glanced around, making a note of the different clicks that seemed to be situated throughout the space. Even without their lanyards, and all the color-coding crap the academy did, it was easy to pinpoint who belonged to what house. Everyone seemed to stick with their own kind.

A group of girls neared us. I felt their eyes on me before they sashayed around where we stood, but I didn't pay them any attention. I wasn't here for that. Every part of me knew it. A tall brunette in the group bumped into me on purpose and nearly fell on her face. I caught her inches before she hit the title floor. She would have been fine if she'd fallen, but it was the principle of the matter. She smiled up at me, batting her heavily coated lashes.

"Thanks," she breathed.

I didn't speak. Instead, I had her in a standing position and my hands off her in two seconds flat. Her heels clicked across the tile floor as she walked away when an awkward silence built between us.

"How do you do that?" Lee asked. When I glanced at him, he wore a baffled expression.

"Do what?"

"Get girls to fall all over you without doing a thing." I could sense hostility in his tone. A slow smile spread across my face. "I mean, that girl practically threw herself at you."

"First of all, I don't go around wearing shit like that." I pointed to his t-shirt. There was a picture of the comic book character he was obsessed with printed on the front in an action pose.

"Low blow, man, low blow. Do you even know how cool this guy is?" He was serious. His face said it all. "He can freaking teleport! That's the coolest power anyone could ever have. You'd save so much money and time teleporting places instead of driving or flying."

"You're right. What was I thinking? What were those girls' thinking?" I asked with mock seriousness hanging in my tone. My grin grew when he rolled his eyes and huffed. I placed a hand on his shoulder to steady him, knowing he was on the verge of walking away. "I'll tell you what they were thinking—they were thinking how their kid brother would wear something like that. They want a man. Not some boy who, based on his clothing choices, they might have to babysit."

"I'm not even going to argue with you on that because I know you're right." He ran a hand through his hair. "It wouldn't be the first time something like that has been said to me."

I laughed. This guy was a trip. He might be nerdy as hell, but I was glad he was my roommate and not someone else's.

"Don't let it get you down. Let's grab something to eat. I'm starved and ready for my free meal." I headed toward the food. It was a little after seven, but the cafeteria still seemed to be open. Lee followed.

The variety of food was as wide as I'd suspected. There was blood, burgers, and everything in between. No one would be going hungry anytime soon. I picked a bag of O positive and a thing of beef jerky while Lee piled his tray with two cheeseburgers and a mountain of fries.

"Damn, don't they feed you wherever you come from?" I teased.

A smirk worked its way onto his face. "Sorry. I haven't eaten much today. Traveling makes me anxious, and I can't eat when I'm anxious. My hunger is catching up with me now."

After we swiped our ID cards, we found a table near the back and sat to eat. Nobody opted to sit with us, though they did glance our way before continuing elsewhere. I was fine with that. I wasn't here to make friends.

As long as I enjoyed the company of my roommate, considering I had to be around him more than anyone else, I was fine.

"Either you're right about my t-shirt and it's shouting nerd way too loud and scaring everyone away, or else it's your muscles and tattoos," Lee said around a mouthful of cheeseburger. I scoffed. "What's up with all the tattoos, anyway? Are you one of those guys who likes pain or something?"

I took a swig from my bag of blood. This guy was observant as hell. That was something I'd noticed about him immediately. Not much had to be said around him for him to get you. Also, if he touched on things I didn't care to talk about, all I had to do was give him a look and he shut his mouth right then.

"Something like that." I surveyed the dining hall, not meeting his stare.

I was looking for something, but I wasn't sure what. Heck, I wasn't even sure which part of me was doing the looking, my wolf or my vampire—but I figured I'd know whenever I saw it.

Lee didn't press the question about my tattoos. I was glad. Tattoos were a personal thing. At least for me. They told the story of my life. The things that ruled me. The moments that lifted me up. The tragedies that broke me down.

Everything in my life that had ever been tattooed on my soul was also on my skin.

"So, beyond the obvious," Lee said after some time

had passed. "Which house do you think you'll hate the most?"

I arched a brow. "Besides the obvious? You already have a problem with one of the houses?"

He wiped his mouth on a napkin and stared at me with big eyes. "Well, yeah. Wolf Bloods and Wolf Bounds never get along. There's always been a household rivalry between the two. It's like ancient or some shit. You didn't know that?"

"Nope. I'm not into ancient drama." In fact, I wasn't into drama at all.

The world would be a better place if more people avoided drama instead of stirring it up.

"I'm not either, but this is just a given. The Wolf Bounds have always thought they were better than us. Witches vs vampires."

I popped a piece of beef jerky in my mouth and shrugged. "Maybe they are."

"I can't believe you just said that." Lee's eyes widened. "If any of the other Wolf Bloods hear you say that, you're going to have a fight on your hands."

My insides tingled, and both my demons surfaced at the mention of a fight. "Really?"

"Hell yeah! To Wolf Bloods, that's an age-old fight right there. Wolf Born and Wolf Bitten have the same rival happening between them too. Have for decades." Lee popped a fry in his mouth. "Not that getting in a fight would bother you. You seem like the type who'd enjoy it."

There he was seeing me for who I am without me

uttering a damn word. Did he know how observant he was?

"You might be right," I said, flashing him a smirk. "But don't worry, I can handle my own."

"Oh, I have no doubt."

I popped my last piece of beef jerky in my mouth and glanced around, sizing up which guys it would be beneficial to start a fight with. Unbeknownst to me, that was exactly what I'd been doing earlier without noticing. While I was here for control, I knew it wasn't going to come easy and it wouldn't be instant. Fighting would be the only way to keep myself in check and to make sure my humanity remained intact.

My gaze drifted from group to group, house to house. The Wolf Borns seemed to all have that invisible chip on their shoulders like the guy I'd seen in the parking lot earlier. I wasn't sure if fighting any of them would be worth my time. Cocky pretty boys were easy to take down. The problem was that it often affected their pride, and they came back for more. Never alone, though. They always brought their friends. The second match was never a fair one. While I enjoyed a good fight, it had to be fair.

One on one. That was how I fought.

I shifted my attention to a group of Wolf Bound guys. My gut told me they might not fight fair either. Thanks to the ancient grudge Lee had mentioned. They might use their magic to their advantage. Yeah, I was almost certain they'd be trickster magicians. That wasn't who I wanted to go against either.

My eyes drifted... until they landed on Faith. Damn, she was gorgeous. Her dark hair, creamy skin, and red painted lips had her standing out from all the other women here.

She glanced at her phone as she made her way farther into the dining hall. Something about her expression struck a chord in me. She didn't seem happy with whatever she saw. Was it a picture? A text? Someone she hated calling? Her chatty friend, Nora, said something to her, and Faith shoved her phone into her back pocket, trying to act like whatever she'd been looking at hadn't shook her up.

It had. I saw it.

A sudden desire to make sure she was okay pulsed through me. My grip tightened on the bag of blood I sipped from as I fought against it.

"What's got you acting all Hulk-like?" Lee asked, noticing I was out of sorts far easier than I would've liked. "Never mind, I see who's got your attention. You should go talk to her." He slapped me on the back.

"Not going to happen."

"Why not? I'm sure you'd have her eating out of the palm of your hand in minutes."

I glared at him. My wolf let out a low growl I knew had my eyes looking wicked, and he held his hands up in surrender.

"Okay. Subject dropped. I won't mention it again." He took a bite of his cheeseburger and shifted his gaze elsewhere.

Against my better judgment, I allowed my eyes to

drift back to Faith. Nora was still going a mile a minute about something while eating a plateful of fries, but Faith seemed to be miles away. Whatever had been on her cell was still occupying her thoughts.

My wolf paced. He wanted to know what was bothering her. I inhaled a deep breath, forcing myself to remain where I was and not give into him. He bucked against me, but I pushed right back.

What was it about this girl that made him want to protect her? To check on her well-being?

My lips twisted into a frown as I realized my vampire seemed to care about her too. She'd gotten under my skin somehow, and we'd barely said more than a handful of words to each other.

The last person who'd been able to do that was... Ansley.

My lungs constricted. Faith was no Ansley. While I might not know much about her, I knew comparing her to Ansley was like comparing night and day. They were exact opposites.

Needing a distraction, I shifted my attention to a cluster of guys talking about something in hushed voices two tables over. My eyes narrowed on them when I noticed they were a table of mixed houses. Hostility, testosterone, and dominance bounced off them all. It rippled through the air and had my wolf perking up. I tried to zero in on what they were saying, but the noise of the room combined with the distance between our tables made it impossible. There were only two words I could pick out of their conversation, but they were the only two I cared to hear.

Fight and club.

Hell yeah. I knew this place would have something like that happening underground. Rule number six might be no fighting, but I knew it would be among the first rules broken. You couldn't put this many werewolves together and not expect a fight or two to occur.

"You about done?" I asked Lee, my eyes still fixed on the table of guys.

"Uh, I got a couple bites left, but I can pound them in a few seconds," he answered around a mouthful of food. "Why? Ready to get out of here?"

"No. I want to talk to those guys." I nodded in their direction. Lee glanced at them, and I watched from the corner of my eye as his back stiffened.

While I knew there was no way he'd stand two seconds up against any of them in a fight, I assumed there would be a few nerdy guys tossed in the mix eventually that he could go against. Most nerdy guys had repressed anger they needed to let go of, and an underground fight club was the perfect place to do it.

Lee needed this as much as I did.

Not because I sensed he had repressed anger, but because he needed some damn confidence in himself. This was a surefire way to get it. Nothing boosted a man's confidence more than kicking someone's ass and gaining respect while doing it. Girls would flock to him then. They loved a bad boy, and nothing screamed bad boy more than someone with a fat lip or a busted nose who'd just won a fight.

Lee snapped his gaze from them back to me. "About what exactly?"

"The underground fight club they're forming."

"Uh, that's not something I care to be a part of for many reasons. Why do you?"

I squeezed his shoulder and flashed him a lopsided grin. "Because it's the only thing that will make sure I don't accidentally rip your head off." I was kidding, but he didn't need to know that. Lee had no reason to fear me, my wolf, or my vampire.

Still, I knew my demons well enough to know they needed an outlet. That they craved it. Hell, I craved it too. Fighting had always been the best outlet I'd found.

Lee put the remaining part of his burger down and wiped his hands on a napkin. "Okay, let's go, then."

"Weren't you planning on pounding that back?" I chuckled as I stood up from my seat and gathered my trash. Lee walked with me to the trash can.

"I'm not hungry anymore."

I glanced at him. He was a little green. I laughed. Yeah, he definitely needed to be part of that club as much as I did. Lee needed to toughen up.

I started toward the table of guys, trying to pinpoint the leader as I walked. If I had to guess, I'd say it was the big guy in the middle with the scar on his face. The dude had to be close to six-foot-seven. He reminded me of a Viking. He was all solid muscle and dark features. I knew right away he was from my house—Wolf Blood—same as

I knew he wasn't someone to screw around with. He'd definitely be the guy to beat, and I was just the guy to try it.

I'd always loved a challenge.

The Viking locked eyes with me as we neared his table. He leaned back in his seat and folded his arms over his chest. Everyone around him fell silent. He skimmed the length of me, sizing me up. I kept my back straight and my jaw set. When the corner of Viking's mouth quirked into a crooked grin, I knew he'd be willing to put me in his club.

"I'd like to join." My gaze never faltered from his as I spoke.

"Join what?" His head tipped to the side, and his eyes grew darker.

My wolf snarled, feeling threatened and challenged at the same time. I imagined it was in reaction to this guy's wolf. He felt strong and oozed dominance.

Excitement burned through my veins.

This was exactly the kind of guy I wanted to go up against. He'd beat the living shit out of me, and I'd love every second of it.

Fighting was the only time I didn't think of those I'd lost because of my actions. It was the only time I could feel something other than the guilt that tormented me.

"Your club. I said I want in. Me and my friend here do." I nodded to Lee standing beside me. "What do we need to do to make it happen?"

Viking laughed. So did some of his friends. I didn't. In fact, I didn't even crack a smile. I kept my eyes locked on his and my jaw set. Viking's eyes drifted to Lee. They raked him up and down. I didn't have to look at Lee to know he didn't seem like this was his type of thing; the guy was wearing a comic character t-shirt and chewing on his thumbnail. Still, I knew he needed to be a part of this.

"You want in this thing?" Viking asked Lee, his smirk growing. "You sure you can handle it?"

When Lee didn't say anything, I nudged him with my elbow.

"Um, maybe?" Lee muttered. I nudged him again, this time harder than before. "Probably. I mean, yeah. Sure. Definitely."

"Now that I'd like to see." One of the guys seated near Viking sneered.

I cut my gaze to him. He wasn't as muscular as the rest of the guys around him, and I was almost positive he was from Wolf Bitten. He didn't seem cocky or overly confident. He looked like he had street smarts though. And, there was a genuine look of amusement reflected in his eyes. He did want to see Lee fight.

So did I.

"Tell us when and where," I said, shifting my attention back to Viking. "We'll be there."

"That's not how this thing works. You don't get that kind of information up front," Viking said, his eyes zeroing in on me. "There's an initiation first."

I licked my lips and allowed the smirk that wanted to form do its thing. "Okay. Well, just know that we're in. Both of us."

I reached out to shake his hand. He chuckled before he gripped my hand tight and shook.

"What's your name?" he asked.

"Axel. Axel Stone."

"Bryant." He released my hand. "You're one ballsy dude. Not many would risk walking up to me and saying they wanted in on anything I had going. I like that."

"Fighting is my thing," I said. It was an understatement.

"And, you are?" Bryant shifted his attention to Lee, holding his hand out for a shake.

"Lee Twain." He reached out to grip his hand. For some reason though, he hesitated right before their palms connected. I didn't know why. All I knew was that something Lee saw had his face growing pale. Lee licked his lips and gave Bryant's hand a squeeze before being the first to release. "Nice to meet you."

"You too." Bryant's brows pinched together. He'd caught Lee's hesitation and could sense his anxiety, same as I could.

I slapped Lee on the back, opting to end the awkwardness shifting between the two of them and get him away from Bryant and his group so I could figure out what the hell had happened.

"All right, well, I guess we'll see you guys around. Don't forget, we want in," I said as I backed away from their table, pulling Lee along with me.

"Noted, brother," Bryant said with a nod of his head. His eyes drifted from me to Lee, and a suspicious gleam dulled their color.

"What the hell happened back there?" I asked Lee once we were outside the dining hall, heading back to our dorm house.

"What?"

I glared at him, making it clear I wasn't playing games. "You know what I'm talking about."

"Nothing." He scratched his neck. "Just something I noticed. It's silly. Really. I don't even know why I reacted the way I did." He shook his head as though attempting to shake away his unease. It didn't work. I could still sense it lingering in the surrounding air.

"I call bullshit. Whatever it was freaked you the fuck out."

"You'll think it's dumb."

"Maybe, but neither of us will know for sure until you tell me."

Lee crammed his hands into the pocket of his jeans and dropped his gaze to the concrete passing beneath his shoes as we walked. "It-it was his tattoo. The one on the skin between his thumb and index finger."

I hadn't even noticed a tattoo. Typically, it was something I scoped out on someone first thing, but only because I respected them as art.

"You freaked out because of a tattoo?" I tried not to laugh, but a smirk twisted my lips, regardless. "What was it of?"

Lee rolled his eyes. "I knew you'd think it was ridiculous. It was a symbol."

"Relax. It was just a tattoo. They don't bite."

"It wasn't the tattoo that freaked me out, not really.

It's what it stands for." His brows pulled together. "At least, I think it was the same one my crazy uncle used to talk about. There was a story that went with it about a secret, ancient group hidden among our kind that called themselves the—"

"You know what?" I held up a hand to stop him from saying more. "You can just stop right there. Sorry, man, but I don't do conspiracy theories."

"All right, fine." Lee scratched his head. "It's just a story, anyway. Maybe that guy was a fan."

"Enough. Let's talk about how we just found out there's an underground fight club and worked our way in." A wide smile spread across my face.

"I've never seen someone so excited about fighting. What if you go against that behemoth of a guy, Bryant?"

My grin grew. My wolf nudged his way to the surface, and I knew my eyes had taken on his golden color. "I'm hoping to."

"You've got a death wish, dude." Lee chuckled with a shake of his head.

I laughed and shoved him. My laughter died out, and the smile melted off my face when I spotted Faith up ahead. She stood with her friend, Nora, and two other girls in the middle of the sidewalk. They were all chatting about something, except for Faith. Tension still radiated off her. When we grew closer to where they stood, Faith lifted her gaze to lock with mine. Her eyes were still distant. Something shone in the depths of their color that had my demons rushing to the surface at the same time.

She was scared of something.

I cut my eyes to the sidewalk and crammed my hands in my pockets, keeping my head down, I passed her and her group. There was no way in hell I'd ask her what had her insides trembling while her outer shell remained intact for everyone to see. No way I'd tell her I saw right through her, right down to the fear and worry that ate away at her insides.

"You should say hi to her. Or maybe *sup, girl*," Lee said in a voice deeper than his own.

"Never make that voice again." I chuckled.

"I'll admit that was bad, but still. There's something between you two. Anyone can see it."

I didn't reply. Instead, I cut into the dorm house, trying like hell not to look back at Faith. It took every ounce of willpower I had because I could feel her eyes on me.

FAITH

*O*rientation had gone entirely too fast. I couldn't believe it was already the second day in the semester. I hurried to the building Nora pointed out yesterday where my Strength Training class was supposed to be held. She'd had the class yesterday and mentioned more than once last night how sore she was. She'd also said Professor Blades was intense. I wasn't shocked. I'd gathered as much during orientation when he stood behind the Wolf Bloods' table, watching everyone sign in with his muscular arms folded over his solid chest.

What surprised me was that it had been three days since Van had sent me the text asking what I'd done. I still hadn't responded. I didn't want to. All I wanted was for that part of my life to leave me alone.

The doors to Strength Training were wide open when I neared them. I spotted a large mat spread out on the hardwood floor. Crap. I hoped we weren't doing some form of martial arts or karate. I sucked at both. What I excelled at was running on a treadmill, using an elliptical, and sit-ups. I could do a million sit-ups without breaking a sweat.

I paused to tie my sneakers outside the double doors. A few others attending class passed me dressed in workout clothes and sneakers, same as me. Some of the tension in my shoulders melted. I was glad there wasn't a uniform I was supposed to wear for this class like the others.

My cell chimed with a new text from inside the secret pocket of my workout pants.

I froze. Shit. That couldn't be Van again. Could it? My heart kick-started inside my chest as I retrieved my phone.

Faith, you can't ignore me forever. What did you do? I can't help unless you tell me.

My thumbs hovered over the keyboard. I wanted to tell him. Hell, I'd wanted to tell him when it happened. The problem was: I wasn't sure he would believe me. I wasn't sure anyone would.

My teeth sank into my bottom lip as I stared at the two text messages from him. How long would it be before he decided to give up on texting and start calling? I could block him. Delete the text messages and block him. Problem solved.

Not really, though. Not with Van.

He'd figure out a way to find me. It wouldn't happen today, but it might soon if I didn't respond. My wolf paced. She felt my emotions and was getting worked up. This was never a good thing.

Someone bumped into me from the side as a group of three girls entered the building.

I shoved my cell back in my secret pocket, deciding I'd handle it later, and followed them in.

The room was larger than I thought it would be. Machines and equipment lined the walls. One was as familiar to me as my bike—the elliptical. I couldn't wait to get on it and work up a sweat. My gaze drifted to a machine beside it. I didn't know what it was called, but I knew what muscles it targeted because I'd used it before —lower abs. That sucker would keep my abs flat as could be. It would also keep a wall to my back, so I didn't have to worry about anyone sneaking up behind me or checking out my ass while I worked out.

I hated this class was co-ed.

I crossed to the center of the room where everyone seemed to congregate. My gaze drifted to the faces surrounding me. There were a few I recognized from my other classes, but only one sent butterflies into flight through my stomach.

Axel.

We hadn't shared any other classes, why did we have to share this one? I was sure to be sweaty and gross daily. The thought of him seeing me that way on a regular occasion had dread uncoiling in the pit of my stomach.

I mentally kicked myself. Why did I even care?

I was swearing off guys. Which meant, him being here shouldn't matter. It also meant that I definitely shouldn't be staring at him, but I was. The white cotton t-shirt he wore was snug around his biceps and chest. It was just see-through enough that I could see the same tattoos covering his arms from the wrist up also spread across his chest and down to the waist of his shorts.

Did they go any lower?

Someone clapped their hands together loudly, gaining the attention of everyone in the room. I was glad because my mind had dipped to places it shouldn't. Professor Blades stood near a door I was sure led to his office. He was even more intimidating than I remembered with his muscles bulging and his dark eyes.

"Listen up. This is strength training. I'm Professor Blades, and this is my domain. You will do as you're told. You will be respectful. And you will do your best at everything within these walls. Understood?"

I nodded like some others while a few said, yes, sir. It was unclear which he preferred. The guy was seriously scary though, and I doubted anyone wanted to piss him off.

"Let's warm up, and then transition into a few circuits."

I'd been expecting this. Nora had filled me in on what her first day of Strength Training had been like. While I hoped mine would be similar, I also was disappointed we wouldn't be using the machines. The amount of pent-up energy I needed to burn was overwhelming, and time on any of them would have helped.

"All right. Line up so I can pair you with someone," Professor Blades said. I watched as he paired one boy with one girl, moving his way down the line. My stomach flipped. Nora had forgot to mention this. "I've learned from the previous classes this week that you'll each do better with a little direct competition. Once you've been assigned your competition, I'll blow my whistle and you can begin doing suicide sprints."

I glanced at the girl beside me. She was tall and all legs. If we were racing each other while doing sprints, she was sure to beat me.

"How many?" someone asked down the line.

"More than my previous classes this week. You can thank that guy for interrupting before I finished pairing everyone."

A collective groan echoed through the room.

Professor Blades reached me. "You and," he said before pointing to someone, "you."

I glanced around the tall girl beside me, checking to see who my competition was. A lump formed in my throat when I saw it was Axel.

This would be my least favorite class. Ever.

"Swap places," Professor Blades prompted Axel and the tall girl beside me.

They switched, and I tried not to focus on how close Axel was to me now, but couldn't. My left side tingled with his nearness. I inhaled a deep breath, hoping to calm the hell down, but all I did was inhale his sexy-smelling cologne.

Oh, sweet Jesus.

Having him as my competition was not going to be

good. I needed distance between us. Which was exactly what I planned on doing.

Axel was going to eat my dust.

I prepared to launch forward, looking at Professor Blades, waiting for him to blow his whistle and signal the start of our suicide sprints. Once he did, I bolted forward. I was at the first line we were supposed to touch with our fingertips and back to our original starting point in seconds.

Axel was right beside me.

Damn him. He could keep up with me easier than I'd thought. I pushed myself harder when I made it to the next line we were supposed to touch. Still, Axel kept up. He wasn't showing any signs of slowing, but then again, neither was I. Being Wolf Blood meant we had great stamina, thanks to our vampire side. And, I was about to tap into it more than I ever had as I pushed myself even harder. Axel did the same. We continued pushing ourselves until Professor Blades finally blew his whistle, signaling the end of our suicide sprints.

Thank, God.

"Well done, everyone." He nodded as he eyed us all one by one. "Let's break for five and get some water."

I leaned over, placing my hands on my knees to catch my breath. My legs felt like Jell-O. My heart pounded, and I couldn't dim the smile that twitched at my lips even if I tried. This was exactly what I needed. An extreme workout to release some of my pent-up energy.

"You're fast," I said when I noticed Axel watching

me. He was bent over too, struggling to catch his breath. "Faster than I thought you'd be."

I shouldn't have said anything to him, but I couldn't help it. The words fell from my brain to my lips beyond my control.

"Same goes for you." He stood to his full height and then lifted the edge of his t-shirt to wipe away the sweat from his face. The action revealed his chiseled abs and tattoos. Holy shit, he had a nice body. My lungs did a weird thing that had me making a strange gasping noise. I averted my eyes before he glanced at me and spotted a few other girls eyeing him. One mouthed the word lucky to me.

Why did she think I was lucky? Because I was paired with him? I would have gladly been paired with any of the other guys, because being paired with Axel was torturing my libido.

I made my way to the water fountain and found a place at the end of the long line. Next class, I'd make sure to bring my own water.

"When you're finished getting water, I want you back over here in the center of the room," Professor Blades said. "We're done with suicide sprints for today. What I'd like you to do next is a friendly push-up challenge." His eyes gleamed with excitement, but they didn't brighten. Not even a smidge. They remained scary dark.

Why couldn't it be sit-ups?

I hated push-ups. Even so, I was down to give Axel a run for his money. There was no doubt he could do more than me, but I'd at least make him work hard for his first few sets. He'd already learned not to underestimate me in the sprint challenge, after all.

When my turn finally came for the fountain, I barely had time to take a sip before Professor Blades announced our break was over. This pissed me off, but I wasn't about to argue with him. Instead, I made my way back to where Axel stood. He took a long swig from a bottle of water. When he finished, he held it out to me.

"Next time, you should think about bringing your own. It did say something like that on the side note beneath where it listed workout clothes and sneakers as the attire for this class," he said with a smirk.

I rolled my eyes as I took the bottle from him. I wanted to deck him, and kiss him.

Damn, I needed help. He was pulling me in so many different directions it was insane.

Professor Blades clapped his hands together. "Push-up challenge time. Here's how this works—I set a timer and you see how many you can get. Your goal is to beat your partner." A shit-eating grin spread across his face. It had me thinking he thought of push-ups as torture, and the idea of torturing us made him smile.

I cringed.

Axel beat me at the push-up challenge, but I creamed him when we did sit-ups next. Shortly after, Professor Blades had us run laps around the room. Then we settled in for mixed martial arts. He claimed martial arts was way better than the yoga crap Professor Trinity taught in her Meditation and Spiritual Release class. I wasn't sure I agreed.

I was halfway through the sequence of moves Professor Blades taught us when my cell vibrated in my secret pocket. Shock jolted threw me, throwing my balance off. I stumbled to the side a few steps.

"You should focus. Not on the phone vibrating in your pocket, but on what you're doing here," Axel insisted as though he were my teacher.

My temper flared. Who the hell was he to tell me what to do? He didn't know me, and he damn sure didn't know what I was up against right now.

"I am focusing. What makes you think I'm not?" I snapped.

Axel shifted to glance at me, making me the center of his attention. It wasn't a place I wanted to be. Not right now. Not like this. Not when he was seeing me for who I was—a hot mess who was scared shitless.

"Besides the fact you nearly fell on your ass two seconds ago, I also can tell when someone is haunted by their past mistakes." His eyes never wavered from me when he spoke.

"Takes one to no one," I tossed back without much thought.

His lips quirked into a smug smirk, but there was sadness in his eyes. "Touché."

For the rest of class, I refused to look at Axel again. I focused on each movement and attempted to control my racing thoughts. All I wanted to do was read my new text. I didn't dare pull my cell out though. Professor Blades would probably crush it with his bare hands and toss it across the room. He'd made it clear multiple times that he didn't like when someone wasted his time, and I knew being on my cell during any point in his class would be considered as such.

The instant I left class, I reached for my cell. When I glanced at the new text from Van, everything I'd worked so hard to push away during Strength Training came rushing back.

If you ever loved me at all, you'll answer me.

My heart pounded. My breath hitched. Shit. He had to go there?

AXEL

The nightmares had returned. I'd been suffering from them the past couple of weeks. In them, all I could see was Ansley's horrified face. All I could hear was her screams. I tried to calm myself down, but couldn't. Everything was red. Everything was too much. My demons pulled me in different directions, leaving me unable to tell which one would win.

And then we crashed.

Her body flew from the passenger seat straight out the windshield. She landed on the brittle grass in front of me. Limp. A delicate flower broken.

And then I woke.

Each time, I bolted upright in bed. My heart pounding. My lungs starving for the air they didn't deserve. And my insides twisted with the guilt that was always just beneath the surface, waiting to torment me. My vampire craved blood. My wolf wanted to shift.

Both of them wanted to fight. Against me. Against each other. Against someone new.

I stared at the ceiling, not knowing what time it was or caring. Images from the nightmare shifted through my mind, a slideshow I couldn't turn away from. I squeezed my eyes shut, but it didn't help. I could still hear the echo of her screams.

My fingers grabbed hold of the promise ring hung from my neck. For the millionth time, I wanted to strangle myself with the necklace, but I knew it wouldn't do any good. Something like that wouldn't kill me. Hell, it probably wouldn't even hurt.

Instead, I did what I always did—I repeated the promise I'd made to her at her funeral.

"I'm here for you. I'm here because of you. I'm here to learn control," I whispered into the dark room.

The promise was easy to stick to because I was committed. The problem was that I hadn't seen any progress in myself the past few weeks, so frustration wasn't far behind when I thought about it.

I'd expected more from myself.

Disappointment surged through me. I rolled over to grab the bag of blood I'd left on the desk earlier and tore the corner open. I chugged its contents to satisfy my vampire. My wolf howled because he wanted something satisfying too.

There was nothing I could give him though. If I shifted in the dorm house, I risked attacking someone. My wolf had already pegged a few on our floor he would love to challenge.

As I tossed the empty bag of blood in the trash, my wolf bucked against me, demanding to be set free. The skin on my arms prickled as his fur struggled to push its way through against my will. I got up and paced the length of the room, hoping I didn't wake Lee. My wolf nipped at me. He was an aggressive bastard tonight.

I ran my fingers through my hair. If I didn't give into him, he might take over and force the change on his own. It had happened before.

When he bucked against me hard enough to bring me to my knees, my decision was made. I'd have to break rule number one and shift when it wasn't sanctioned. I couldn't hold out any longer.

Even without the nightmares, my wolf would have needed to shift—to run—soon. There was too much here causing him to bristle.

Faith, and her gorgeous body, was one of them. And, that damn coconut vanilla scent she wore. That was what was driving my wolf to his breaking point lately.

I picked up my jeans from the floor and put them on. My ID was still in the back pocket. Next, I slipped on my boots, and then grabbed a shirt and cracked the door open to let myself out. My eyes drifted to Lee before I closed the door behind me. He was still sawing logs, hugging his pillow.

Creeping through the Wolf Blood dormitory at night was eerie. Mainly because I knew I wasn't the only one wide-awake. Others were staring at their ceilings or screwing around on their cell phones. Noises sounded from a few of the rooms as I passed, but I didn't pause. I kept walking toward the stairs. Once I made it down the four flights, I paused. There were people in the main lounge. A few were playing pool. I could hear the balls cracking as someone broke the setup. I chewed the inside of my cheek and headed for the door, hoping like hell no one saw me and claimed I wasn't allowed out of the house past a certain hour because I knew my wolf would free himself and tear into whoever it was. I wouldn't be able to stop him.

Once I stepped outside, the thrill of what I was about to do sank in.

I was about to shift.

The woods in the distance came into view after a few steps, and I quickened my pace. They called to me. My heart pumped hard and fast as anticipation rushed through my veins.

I felt alive, and both my demons loved the sensation.

I soon broke into a jog, feeling as eager as my wolf to shift. Not shifting had been hell for both of us. It left me unbalanced. Normally, I shifted daily. If that wasn't possible, then I damn sure shifted every other day. That was the only way to keep my wolf happy. Same as feeding daily was the only way to keep my vampire happy. It was how I worked. Take either away and my sanity suffered.

This was where I was at. It was why the nightmares had started again. I needed to find my balance. My emotions couldn't be out of whack at the same time my demons were being deprived. That was when shit went crazy.

That was when I went crazy.

As I crept deeper into the woods, I tried to pinpoint what might have triggered the nightmares of Ansley to start up again. Was it being at Lunar Academy and all the stress that went with it? Was it not being able to shift like I normally would? Or was it something else? Someone else, maybe?

Faith popped in my head.

My body jolted to a stop. It was her. She was the reason my nightmares had returned. There were too many similarities between her and Ansley I'd noticed lately. I'd made a mistake in thinking they were like night and day, but they weren't. Time had shown as much to me.

Images of both flashed through my mind.

The way they carried themselves. Their creamy skin. The way they looked at me—as though they knew I was dangerous, but didn't give a shit.

My wolf howled, begging me to set him free. I didn't fight him, not this time. Besides, I couldn't even if I tried. I was disgusted with myself. I'd just compared a girl I barely knew to Ansley. My Ansley.

I peeled off my clothes in a hurry and tossed them to the forest floor.

My wolf broke free. His fur forced its way through my pores. My bones bent and broke, morphing into his form. The force of the shift was primal. It was raw and emotional.

It was me running from both my past and present.

My skin rippled one last time as my wolf finished his

swift change. I let my mind wander as he took over. His paws scratched at the ground, his excitement getting the best of him. The damp scent of earth filled our snout, and I fully expected him to let out a howl, but he didn't. He knew it might alert someone to us, and then we'd be in trouble. Instead, he bolted through the woods, running full speed. Leaves and debris kicked up behind us.

All was right... until he caught the scent of another wolf lingering in the air.

My wolf came to a halt. He pulled in a deep breath, gaining as much information about the other wolf as the air could hold—male, heavily dominant, slightly older, and... close by.

I nudged my wolf to the side. Not fully, but enough to let him know I was paying attention. I'd have to take over soon. If I didn't put him back in his corner, he'd track down the other wolf and fight for this territory. It was in his nature. My wolf was as much of a fighter as I was. If that happened, there was no way I would be able to rein him in, and then I'd definitely be up shit creek without a paddle when it came to the trouble I'd be in.

He seemed to understand that he was at risk of being shoved to the side and made his way back the way we came. Still, I could tell how worked up he was. Questions tumbled through my mind about whether we'd been followed. When we reached the area where I'd stripped, I forced my wolf back into his corner. He didn't go easily because of the potent scent of the other wolf in the air here.

Shit. Had someone followed me?

Once my shift was complete, I quickly dressed. The other wolf could be anyone—a teacher or student. Hell, it could be a werewolf security guard who patrolled the academy at night. I had no clue if that was even a thing, but it might be. They had to enforce the rules somehow, right? I just hadn't seen anyone do it yet.

I pulled my boots on and jogged to the edge of the woods. When I reached them, I glanced around, searching for anyone who might see me. There didn't seem to be anyone around. I exited the woods and made a move to cut across campus to the Wolf Blood dormitory, but something caught my eye. No, not something... someone.

There was someone leaning against the building, shrouded in shadows. I could feel their eyes on me. As I neared, I took note of their height and build. A low chuckle slipped from the guy, and it was all I needed to know who it was watching me.

Bryant.

My wolf bristled with excitement. My vampire stared with suspicion, his fangs ready to fall. Was this how I got the official invitation to join fight club, or was this when the initiation would take place? I continued toward him, ready to find out.

As I neared him, it became easier to see his face. A smirk twisted his features.

"Out for a midnight run, I see," he said.

"The same could be said about you." I instinctively knew the wolf in the woods with me had been him. I could sense it.

"True. One of the things about this place is that they don't give you enough sanctioned run times. And even if they did, they're all in packs. For those who prefer to be alone in wolf form, it's a bit of a raw deal."

It was unsettling the way he seemed to know this about me. Either he was observant as hell, or he'd been watching me.

I wasn't sure I liked either scenario.

Bryant pushed himself off the wall. His arms remained folded across his chest. The dude was taller than I'd thought, more ripped too, but I still wouldn't back down from a fight against him if that was where this was about to lead. "I figured you were a rule breaker, though."

The light hit his scar just right, and I tried not to stare.

"What gave you that idea?" My hands flexed into fists at my sides, ready to throw a punch if needed.

"I can sense it in you. Takes one to know one sort of thing. And then there's fight club."

"About that," I said, trying my best to keep my attention on him while still paying close attention to my surroundings. In situations like this, you never knew if someone might jump out at you and start a fight. This wasn't the first fight club I'd been a part of. I knew how things worked. "I'm still waiting on my invitation to my first fight. So is my roommate, Lee. Is this thing happening, or what?"

Bryant laughed. "Listen to you. Of course it's happening. These things take time. We have to scope out all candidates first. Especially the ones that come to us instead of us to them." He arched a brow. "Gotta vet you first."

So, he had been watching me.

"Did I make the cut?" I was curious to know.

"Maybe. Maybe not," he said before walking away.

I pulled in a deep breath and hesitated before I followed him into the Wolf Blood house. My demons wanted me to make sure we weren't about to be jumped first. When nothing happened, I headed inside. Bryant wasn't hanging around the main lounge like I thought he might be. Relief trickled through me. Now that my wolf had his fun, I was exhausted.

A light was on inside my dorm room when I reached the door. I grabbed my ID and inserted it. When I swung the door open, Lee was seated at the desk, hunched over his cell, scribbling on a notepad. I closed the door behind me, and slipped off my boots.

"Couldn't sleep either I take it?" I made my way to my dresser for a change of clothes. I knew these reeked of the woods and the change. I could smell it on me.

"Nope." The edge to his tone made me pause. "But you don't see me going off, breaking rules because of it."

I smirked at him. "Breaking rules?" I was eager to hear what he thought I'd done. He seemed worked up.

He shifted in his chair to glare at me. "Yeah, breaking rules. Don't even try to deny it, dude. You reek of woods and having shifted recently."

I held my hands up, waving my athletic shorts in the air as a flag of surrender. "Yeah, I shifted. So sue me. I don't understand why you're pissed about it. It's not like I forced you into going with me."

"You didn't, but you might as well have."

My brows pinched together. "What does that mean?"

"It means that whenever whoever the hell in charge of checking these things out comes asking who it was shifting in the middle of the night during an unsanctioned time, I'm going to have to lie. I'll have to pretend I don't know it was you. You've put me in that position. You and your selfish ways."

Jesus. He was freaking out. I didn't understand where his hostility was coming from. Who the hell cared if someone asked who had snuck out and shifted? Saying you didn't know was a simple lie. It wasn't like they would be able to know. It wasn't like they were going to go door-to-door asking either. At least I didn't think they would.

"I'm not asking you to cover for me." I grabbed a clean shirt and a towel. "And, I don't think anyone will be able to pinpoint it was me in the woods tonight unless someone saw me come in. Even so, I doubt they'd ask you. Besides, I wasn't the only one out there tonight." I started toward the door, ready to head to the communal showers.

"Great. So, somebody probably does know it was you, and you're going to get in trouble for it. Awesome. Then when you get kicked out, I'll get another roommate who won't be half as cool as you are."

I flashed him a smirk from over my shoulder as I gripped the doorknob. "You think I'm cool? Aw, little buddy. So, that's what this is all about? You're worried I'll be canned, and you'll get some shitty new roommate?"

"Don't let it go to your head." Lee rolled his eyes. "But, yeah. Plus, I'm starting to think of you as a friend and I don't want you getting in trouble. Can you please just abide by the damn rules?"

"Says the guy who opted into joining an underground fight club with me, which also breaks the rules." My grin grew, because I knew my comment would get under his skin.

"Hey, you practically twisted my arm about that."

"Keep telling yourself that, and maybe you'll believe it." I chuckled. "You want to join almost as much as I do. A busted-up face gains attention from the women. Trust me. I know from personal experience."

It would also help him gain confidence in himself, but I left that part out. It was something he would have to learn on his own, not something anyone could tell him because he wouldn't believe it.

"I'm not getting into this with you." Lee shook his head, although amusement shone in his eyes. He liked what I said, even if he didn't want to admit it. "Go take a shower, dude. You stink."

"Yeah, yeah. Go back to drawing your comic book characters, or whatever the hell it is you're doing over there." I stepped out into the hall. Lee said something under his breath, but all I heard was the word research.

What the hell was he researching? None of my professors had given out an assignment.

FAITH

I answered the text. How could I not? He'd said *if I ever loved him*. I had loved him. Deeply. For a time. My gaze drifted over the words I replied with.

I'm fine. Leave it alone. Leave me alone.

Admittedly, it wasn't the nicest thing I could have said, but it was what needed to be said because it was what needed to be done. Van needed to drop it. I knew he wouldn't, though. There wasn't anything I could say or do that would make him.

I knew this—I accepted it—but that didn't mean I liked it.

My teeth sank into my bottom lip as I worried over what his next response might be. I knew one was coming. It had been hours since I'd sent mine. Radio silence wasn't something Van did. Unless he was up to one of two things—digging deeper into the whole situation to uproot the truth or he was coming for me.

"Why don't you call whoever it is you're waiting to hear from?" Nora asked. She was on her bed, typing away on her laptop. "It would be better than torturing yourself, wondering when they'll reply. That is what you're doing, right?" She glanced at me.

I let out a sigh. "Yes, but I can't call."

"Why not?"

"I just can't."

I didn't care to elaborate. Telling her I wasn't ready to hear his voice again would open a can of worms. She'd have too many questions I knew I wouldn't be able to answer.

The nail polish along the corner of my middle finger chipped as I worked my fingers, a nervous habit I'd always had. I tossed my cell onto my bed and rolled to my side, so I could reach under the bed for my red fingernail polish. It was third in the line of bottles I stored there. As I shook it, I leaned back against my pillow. My gaze drifted to my cell beside me. Maybe just this once Van would listen to me; maybe he really would do as I asked.

The aroma of fingernail polish floated through the air when I opened the bottle. It was a scent some hated, but one I loved. I fixed the chip in my nail and then blew on it after closing the bottle. The sight of my nail being perfect again settled some panic in me. Keeping my outside looking perfect fooled people. It kept them from seeing what a hot mess I really was inside. If I didn't let it show, they didn't think anything was wrong, and then they had no reason to ask.

"What are you working on? Did one of your professors give you an assignment already?" I asked, glancing at her. I hoped the conversation would distract me from my thoughts—from my past. "None of mine have given me anything yet. Well, Professor Trinity told us to meditate nightly for five minutes, but it's not mandatory. I haven't been doing it. I've learned meditation isn't for me."

Purposely being in my head for any extended period wasn't high on my agenda lately.

"It's not for class. I told you I like to read, but what I didn't tell you is that I'm a book blogger." Excitement festered in Nora's eyes as she glanced at me to gauge my expression.

"What's a book blogger? You mean, you blog about books?"

"Yup." Her attention shifted back to her laptop, and she resumed typing.

"Do you tell the people on your blog every detail of the story?" I asked only because she'd been typing for a solid twenty minutes. I couldn't imagine having more than two sentences to say about a book once I finished reading it. I mean, either you liked it or you didn't.

"No. I talk about what I liked. What I didn't, if anything. Who my favorite character was. If I thought the romance was realistic. There are lots of different things I put into each post. Sometimes I'll even add a few quotes from the book that resonated with me or made me laugh."

I placed my nail polish back beneath my bed and then stood to grab my lipstick from on top of my dresser. "Does the author ever read your review?" I asked as I walked to the mirror hung on the inside of our closet door to touch up my lipstick.

"Most of them."

"Do you get anything for reviewing their book? Like do they compensate you?" I had no idea how this worked, but the conversation was keeping my mind away from Van.

Well, for the most part.

Nora's eyes bugged. I saw it clearly in the mirror. "No. I mean some might send me a signed bookmark or an advanced reader copy of their next book in the series, but I don't do it for money. I do it because I love the author and the worlds they create, and I want to share their books with others. I enjoy supporting authors." She closed her laptop and stared at me. Even if I hadn't been able to see her reflection in the mirror, I would've felt her eyes on me. "I guess I should get ready for class too. What's your first one today?"

I pressed my lips together, blending the bright red in and giving them a matte finish. "Introduction to Moon Phases."

It was the one class I was most excited about. That, and Werewolf History. Learning about my werewolf side was one of the main reasons I was here, besides going into hiding. If I wanted to be a full-fledged Wolf Blood, then I needed to be in tune with my wolf like I was with my vampire. So far, my wolf was just an unpredictable, wild side of me. Having been raised by a vampire nest and my vampire mother, and never having been around many werewolves before, was to blame.

My wolf didn't know how to act.

I figured this place was where we could learn together how werewolves were supposed to behave. This place was supposed to help me find balance. At least, that was the hope.

Nora slipped out of bed and stepped to her dresser where she grabbed her shower caddy and the change of clothes she'd set out the night before. She was so organized it was bordering on being OCD. "I have Wolf Blood Essentials One. Not exactly sure what the syllabus for today will be, but I imagine it will have something to do with learning control over both our sides."

"You'd think." I smoothed my eyebrows, making sure not a hair was out of place. "I have that class later today."

Nora slipped out of the room to head to the communal showers, and I stepped to where my phone still sat on my bed. Why was I waiting on pins and needles for Van to text? I'd told him to leave me alone.

Would it be so bad if he listened?

INTRODUCTION TO MOON Phases had been okay. It wasn't my favorite, but I'd gained some new knowledge today. I still felt disappointed though. It wasn't going to be as hands-on or in-depth as I'd thought it would. Maybe, it was because it was only a first-year class.

On my way to Wolf Blood Essentials, I popped the top on the drink I'd grabbed earlier from a vending machine at the dorm house as I walked. It was practically midday, and the sun was shining bright. There was a slight chill to the air, but it was welcomed. A girl I remembered from one of my classes gave me a wave as we passed one another, and I smiled in response. Being here, at the academy, felt good. It was crazy to think this would be my typical day from here on out until I graduated.

I was okay with it though. Choosing to come here had been one of the best decisions I'd ever made.

When I stepped into the classroom, I made my way to my usual desk in the back. The seats filled up as more entered the room. I was recognizing faces and remembering their names. My gaze drifted to the door, watching as more of my peers filed into the room. Axel's nerdy roommate entered then. He started toward the desk beside me. I groaned, without knowing why. He wasn't Axel. He hadn't even chosen the guy to be his roommate; he'd been assigned to him.

I should cut him some slack.

"Hey. How's it going?" he asked, same as he did every day as he situated himself in the desk beside me. "Hope your day has been better than mine so far." He unzipped his bookbag and fished around inside before pulling out a notebook and pen.

"Not having luck with your first few classes today?"

"She speaks." His eyes widened in mock surprise. I rolled my eyes and flashed him a small smile. "And, not really. My last class was Werewolf History. I'm a huge history buff, so I sort of contradicted some things the professor mentioned. He didn't seem to care for it, but his views seem to be a little one-sided."

"So, you were butting heads with him the entire period I take it, then?"

"Absolutely." His grin widened. There was a sense of pride reflected in his features.

"Good morning, class," Professor Erma said. "Our focus for today's class will be learning the roots to your vampire side. We'll be busting the myths and rumors surrounding vampires, discussing vampire traditions..."

I tuned her out. If this was all the class would be about, then I didn't see why I was here. I knew all of this. Hell, I could probably teach the class. A nest raised me for crying out loud. One that only stuck to traditional vampire ways. My mother didn't even come out during sunlight hours—though she could—because she was that hardcore.

"Let me guess, vampires raised you," Lee said, surprising me. Was I that transparent?

If so, I needed to get my shit together.

"How did you know?"

"Your body language said it all. Plus, I've suspected as much for a while now."

I arched a brow. "My body language?"

"Yeah. You rolled your eyes and let out a little huff while leaning back in your seat and folding your arms over your chest. That's body language for being uninterested. I see it a lot from the female population." His cheeks reddened at his joke.

I wanted to laugh. The chuckle built in the back of my throat, but I didn't release it, because I didn't want to embarrass him more than he already was.

"You're observant," I said instead.

"That I am." He jotted down something the professor had said on his pad of paper, and then shifted his attention back to me. "Which parent of yours was the vampire?"

Normally, I wouldn't have answered a question like that, but something about Lee made me feel comfortable. I liked talking with him. It made me feel guilty for not having done so sooner.

"My mom," I answered.

The corner of his lips twisted into a satisfied smile. It let me know he'd been right in his assumption. "Was she a traditionalist?"

I rolled my eyes. "Yep. Her entire nest was."

"I figured you'd say she had a nest. Most traditionalists do. It's funny though, because back in the day, vampires were solitary creatures. They didn't have nests. They didn't stay with their bloodline or creator either. They roamed the Earth alone."

"Back in the day?" I chuckled.

"You know what I mean."

I opened my mouth to say something in response, but the professor called us out for speaking. Lee immediately apologized. I remained mute while holding her stare. She had my attention, but I wouldn't apologize for having a conversation—especially not one that pertained to her class.

Time ticked on. By the end of the class, Lee had pages of notes and I didn't have a single word. I had no idea what he'd jotted down—or what half the others in class had—there had been nothing said that I felt was important enough to write down. Everything the professor talked about, I already knew. Notes would have been pointless.

"You have lunch next, right?" Lee asked as he gathered his things.

I glanced at him and smiled. He had this lost puppy look festering in his eyes. It was cute. "I do. So does my roommate, Nora. Do you want to sit with us?"

"If you don't mind." He flashed me a lopsided grin as he shifted his books in his arms. Why he didn't put them in his backpack was beyond me. "I'm tired of sitting alone."

"Axel doesn't have this lunch?" I asked even though I already knew the answer. Lee shook his head. "Would he sit with you if he did?" It was a joke, but the look on Lee's face let me know it wasn't a funny one.

"He might look like a tough guy—and he is—but he's a good guy. I'm not sure what's in his past, but I know whatever it is, it haunts him. He's broken by it. I feel for him, so don't make jokes about him, okay?"

I swallowed hard. Weren't we all a little haunted and broken by our past?

"I didn't say that, though," Lee was quick to add. "He'd probably kill me if he knew I said that about him, especially to you."

I gave him a look. "Especially to me, huh?"

I was playing with fire. I knew exactly what he'd meant, and didn't know why I was egging it on. Axel reminded me too much of Van. Especially now that I knew for certain he was haunted by his past. He would be another guy who unintentionally made me fall in love with them while using me, and then I'd be the one to get hurt in the end.

Again.

"Yeah, I'm pretty sure you're his type even if he isn't ready to admit it to himself yet. To be honest, he seems a little lost." Lee scrunched up his face. "I didn't say that either. I really need to shut my mouth."

Satisfaction slithered through me at the thought of being Axel's type. I stomped it out though. It wasn't something I should feel. Not for him. Not for anyone.

Not right now at least. I had bigger things to focus on... like my past.

"Don't worry, I won't say anything." It was the truth. I didn't have any intentions of talking to Axel again. It was best if I kept my distance from him. He would only lead to more heartache and inner turmoil. And, I'd already had enough of that to last me a lifetime.

"Thanks," Lee said as we entered the student center where the dining hall was.

It was a decent-sized room filled with tables and chairs. The place was busy, but I found a few open tables. I spotted Nora next. She stood in line, waving her arms frantically at me while she waited to pay for her lunch.

"And, there's Nora." I started in her direction. Lee chuckled as he walked with me.

"Is she always so energetic?"

"Yup."

"Faith, oh my gosh! You won't believe what

happened," Nora said as soon as we reached her. She slipped out of line to follow me while I checked out the selection of food offered today. "After my last class, I had a few minutes to kill before lunch since my professor let us out early, so I swung by the library. I spotted a poster for the school newsletter on the bulletin board. The description said they were looking for someone to recommend books and write up reviews of popular titles for it. You know how much I love to read. It's like this position was made for me!"

"That's awesome," I said, feeling genuinely happy for her.

"I know, right?" Her eyes widened when I thought they couldn't any more. "I immediately asked the librarian about it. I told her about my blog and everything. She looked me up while I browsed the library's selection and then came to find me. I got the position! It doesn't pay anything, but it's still exciting."

"Congratulations! When does the first newsletter go out?" I asked while I piled a pasta salad with grilled chicken onto my tray.

"You'll have to give me the link for it. I can spread the word about it. I'm into reading too," Lee insisted, sounding a little too enthusiastic. It was clear he thought Nora was attractive.

A grin twisted at my lips. They'd be the cutest nerdy couple at the academy.

Nora looked at Lee as though having just now noticed his presence. "Uh, yeah. I will. Thanks." She stepped behind two people waiting to pay. Her attention bounced back and forth between Lee and me. It was clear I had some explaining to do later.

I grabbed a twelve-ounce can of O positive and added it to my tray. It was synthetic, like all the other blood on campus, but I didn't care. I compared it to drinking vitamin water—it was still water, which was something your body needed to survive, but it was filled with vitamins and minerals your body also needed, giving it an extra boost.

Synthetic blood was no different.

Once both Lee and I had gotten what we wanted and paid, we found Nora at a table off to the side, but still in the thick of things. I would have preferred to sit near the back of the dining hall, so I could people watch, but one glance made me realize there wasn't another table available.

Silence bloomed between the three of us after Lee and I were situated at the table. I could feel Nora's eyes on me, but I didn't look up. I knew she was wondering why he was sitting with us.

"So, which class has been your favorite so far?" Lee asked, breaking up the awkward silence as his eyes bounced between the two of us.

"Meditation and Spiritual Release, I think," Nora answered before I could.

"Really? Are you into all that yoga and meditation stuff?" Lee wrinkled his nose. Obviously, neither were his thing.

"Sort of." Nora shrugged. She stuck a straw into her can of blood. O positive for the win today. All three of us had picked it. "I like silence, so meditation isn't a big deal for me. I could sit in silence for hours and not feel restless. And, yoga has turned out to be more relaxing than I thought it would. Stretching my muscles feels good."

I listened to them holding a conversation together and couldn't help but smile as I again thought they would be a cute couple.

"I don't mind silence. Or stretching. Maybe it was my teacher. She seemed too wound up to teach the class, like she'd had too much coffee." Lee popped a slice of bacon from his BLT into his mouth and chewed. "What about you?" He nodded to me.

"Moon Phases has been cool." Or at least I thought it would be once we got further into the curriculum.

A commotion broke out behind me. I glanced over my shoulder to see what was going on. Two guys seemed ready to go at it, but their friends' pulled them apart.

"Got to watch out for those in Wolf Bitten," Lee said, drawing my attention back to him. "They're like ticking time bombs waiting to explode. I mean it. You should've seen some of them playing basketball yesterday. You would've thought they were going to go to war with each other over a freaking foul."

"I think there are people like that in all the houses," Nora insisted. "You can't put a bunch of werewolves in one place and not expect them to fight or be hostile with each other in some way. Especially when some have hybrid sides and others don't."

I'd often thought the same.

Lee looked like he was about to say something, but

the sight of something—no, someone—had him clamping his mouth shut. I followed his gaze. He was staring at a guy who looked like a Viking near the back of the room. He had solid muscles and dark eyes that were fixed on Lee. He nodded toward the exit and then left the dining hall.

What was that about? Did Lee know him?

"Pretty sure that guy wants to talk to you. What's his deal?" I asked Lee. When he didn't speak right away, I glanced at him. The look on his face made it clear he didn't want to be anywhere near the guy. He looked scared of him. "Hey. What's going on?"

"Nothing. He just wants to talk." Lee didn't meet my stare as he gathered his half-eaten lunch and stood. "Thanks for letting me eat with you two. I'm sure I'll see you both around."

He left the table before either of us could say another word. I could sense his nerves in the air, that and something else—fear. What was he afraid of? That guy, or what the guy might do to him?

I stared after Lee, watching him until he disappeared through the dining hall doors. What the hell had he gotten himself into already? We'd only been at the academy for a few weeks.

AXEL

*I*t was my last class of the day, and honestly, I couldn't wait for it to be over. I wanted out of my scratchy uniform. Well-worn jeans and a plain cotton t-shirt were the only uniform I ever wanted to wear. Button-downs and ties weren't my thing.

I stepped into Meditation and Spiritual Release. The teacher was a little woo-woo, but she was growing on me.

Somewhat.

As I entered the large classroom, I noticed the back doors were open as usual, but instead of the grassy area being empty, everyone sat on tiny pillows with their legs crossed and their palms facing up on their knees.

Shit. Was this the meditation part? Yoga I could handle. I didn't have to think too much about it. All I had to do was exactly as Professor Trinity did and listen to the tinkling music. While down dog wasn't my favorite position—I mean, who really wanted their ass in the air like that for an extended period of time—I managed.

Meditation. Quieting my mind. Sitting in silence for an undetermined length of time.

That I couldn't handle.

There would be no noise to quiet my inner demons. No noise to quiet my thoughts, and the voices that came with them. It would just be me and my memories.

Which sounded like hell.

My palms grew sweaty as I stepped farther into the room. Professor Trinity motioned for me to grab one of the tiny pillows and make myself comfortable on the grassy area with the others.

"Loosen your tie, roll up your sleeves, kick off your shoes," she said as I chose a gray round pillow to sit on, and stepped through the open doors into the sunshiny area. "Relax. Relax your mind. Relax your body. Relax your breath."

I fought the urge to roll my eyes as I made my way to the back of the grassy section. If I did this, it wasn't going to be up in front or in the middle where everyone could stare at me.

The sound of wind chimes blowing in an unfelt breeze floated to my ears.

I had no clue where it came from. It had to be done with magic, because there were no speakers from what I could see. Again, I wondered if Professor Trinity was from Wolf Bound. She was a hard person to read. Her hippie-dippy ways made it impossible to distinguish which house she was from. She didn't color code herself like everyone else either. She'd said during the first class that she didn't believe in it. She claimed segregating us by breed type was a perfect way to create hostility instead of uniting us as one.

I agreed with her. Also, I hated this fucking uniform.

Professor Trinity stepped into the grassy area with us as the last person entered the room. "Please have a seat. Close your eyes. Relax your jaw. And, focus on your breath."

I tossed my pillow on the grass, kicked off my shoes, and rolled up the sleeves of my white button-down before loosening my tie.

I could already feel myself relax.

I crossed my legs like the others, but I didn't close my eyes right away. Instead, I took stock of where everyone else was first. It was an old habit I found hard to break. I always knew the placement of people in my surroundings when I was in a state of vulnerability—like sitting with my eyes closed. Once I felt as though those around me were relaxed enough and in the zone themselves, I closed my eyes and tried to slip into the zone. I focused on my breathing—the way it flowed through my lungs, forcing them to expand and contract—like Professor Trinity said. As soon as I felt I was doing it right, a piece of paper appeared in the palm of my hand out of thin air.

I jolted at the feel, opening my eyes.

My gaze drifted to the others around me. Everyone seemed to be in their own state of meditational bliss.

Who'd given me the paper, then?

I glanced at Professor Trinity, taking note to her position and making sure she wasn't paying attention to me now that I'd opened my eyes. She wasn't. Her eyes were closed, and her head was tilted toward the sky, the slight curve to her lips let me know she was locked in that perfect state of bliss she always talked about. I unfolded the piece of paper and the scent of magic floated to my nose. It was strange and unfamiliar, but magical nonetheless; there was no mistaking it. Words were written in thick, bold lettering. I read them.

Woods. Midnight. And so it begins.

As soon as I read the words, the paper disintegrated in the palm of my hand. In seconds, the only trace of it left behind was the lingering scent of magic across my palm. I thought about what the paper said and smiled.

Anticipation burned through my veins. Come midnight, I'd be duking it out with someone who better know how to throw a fucking punch. I closed my eyes, and for the first time since arriving at the academy, felt more zen and in control of myself than ever before.

LEE SAT AT THE DESK, hunched over whatever he'd been researching forever when I stepped into our dorm.

"Hey, man, did you get an invite for tonight by chance?" I loosened my tie as I crossed to my bed.

"Yeah." He barely glanced at me.

I cracked a grin as I tossed my tie on my bed, and then unbuttoned my starchy button-down. "Jesus, dude.

Don't sound too excited. I know it's not your thing, but you think you could be a bit more pumped than that?"

"I am. I mean, I guess I'm as pumped as anyone can be knowing they're about to get the shit beat out of them for fun." Lee sighed and leaned back in his chair. His fingers ran through his hair, and I knew something was up. He'd been acting strange lately, obsessive with whatever he was researching. "I just... I don't know. I've got a bad feeling about this."

"You've got a case of nerves." I didn't understand it, because it wasn't something I'd ever experienced myself, but I didn't say that. I tried to be supportive. "You'll be okay. You just need to go out there and start throwing punches." It was true. Once you got the first punch in, the rest was a blur.

Anticipation leaked through my veins, bringing my heart rate up and making me look even more forward to tonight's events.

Lee let out another sigh. He picked up the pen he'd been jotting down notes with and tapped it against the desk. "I know. I'm not scared. I just have a bad feeling about Bryant."

I undid my slacks and slipped them off before I reached for my worn jeans on the floor. "Why? Because of his tattoo?" I teased.

"Yeah." He flashed me a look that said go to hell.

I buttoned my jeans and then held up my hands in surrender. "Sorry, I just don't understand why you're flipping out over a tattoo. Is he in a gang you're scared of?"

Was that even a thing? It probably was, but who

knew. Maybe I should've went with the word pack instead. Rival packs were everywhere.

"No. More like a pack, or a clan."

Shit. He was serious. I could tell from the way his brows pinched together and his eyes dipped back to the research he'd been doing. Was he researching the tattoo?

"What have you heard?" I asked, curious for more details. If Bryant was part of something like that, then it might be good to know a few things about the group before getting mixed up with them.

Lee shook his head. "Nothing. It's stupid. Don't worry about it. All I'm saying is I don't have a good feeling about him. I think he's shady."

"I think you're right. He doesn't seem like a trustworthy character on all fronts, but I think he's all right when it comes to fight club." I wasn't sure why I was putting so much trust in him or this situation, but I was going with my gut on it.

Bryant seemed as though respect and rules—to a certain extent—were important to him.

"I'll be there at midnight though," Lee said. His unease leaked through his words. Nothing a little liquid courage couldn't fix. Maybe we should head to Last Call for a drink first.

"Damn right you will. I'm not letting you weasel out of this. I think it'll be good for you." I slapped him on the back and flashed him a smile before pulling my t-shirt over my head. "All right, now that I'm changed, I'm going to head to the dining hall for something to eat. Want to come?"

"I don't know why you hate the uniform so much. It's really not as uncomfortable as you make it seem." He smoothed a hand down his shirt. "Also, it makes me feel fancy. Especially the tie."

I laughed and shook my head. "Something isn't right with you."

"Whatever." Lee stood and pocketed his phone. "Sure, I'll head down with you. Try not to slam the door behind you this time, though. Each time you do, it jars my special card in the closet and knocks it over." He nodded toward where it was in the closet.

I rolled my eyes. Him and his damn comic crap. It was like rooming with a kid.

"I'll try."

We stepped into the hall and made our way to the staircase. I crammed my hands in my pockets as I maneuvered through the crowd in the hall. Everyone seemed to be making a mad rush for the stairs too.

"Oh, I forgot to tell you, I ate lunch with your girl today," Lee said as we started down the first flight of stairs.

"My girl?" I knew who he was talking about, but I tried to pretend I didn't.

"Oh, come on. Don't act like you don't know who I'm talking about."

His words didn't faze me. I continued to do just that —act as though I had no fucking clue who he was talking about.

"Anyway, she's in my essential class—like I've said before—which means we also share lunch. I ate with her and Nora today. She's actually a really cool chick. I think the two of you would be a great couple, if you both would let go of your past a little."

I wanted to ask him what he meant by that. I had sensed something broken in Faith. Hell, I'd said so to her before. There was a part of me that wanted to know what had broken her. I'd never ask though. I knew better than anyone a person would tell you their story when they damn well felt like it and not a second sooner.

Even if you asked.

"Cool," I said, using my nonchalant voice. I didn't make eye contact with him, even though I could feel his gaze on me. "But, the two of us getting together isn't going to happen."

"Sure it isn't," he said in a sing-song voice.

I huffed at him. Two more flights to go, and then we were finally at ground level. Hopefully, this conversation would be over before then.

"Her roommate, Nora, is cool too," he said after a little while.

I glanced at him. "You're into her. Aren't you?"

He shrugged. "She's cute. Smart. A little neurotic, but funny. And, she likes to read. I know comic books aren't necessarily your standard paperback, but it is something we sort of have in common. I do read my comics. I don't just get them to look at the pictures."

"Says every guy who's ever been busted holding a dirty magazine before." I winked. "Sure you read the comics. You don't just get it for the pictures. Uh-huh."

"That was a good one," some guy behind us said,

offering me a fist bump. I'd seen him around campus before and knew he wasn't a first year like the rest of us. He must've started down the steps behind us from one of the previous floors.

Would he be who I was fighting tonight?

If so, I was confident I could take him. He was muscular, but not overly so. A few inches shorter than me. And had a hipster vibe about him. He was dressed in skinny jeans and a cotton t-shirt. With long hair and an ugly as sin pair of shoes on, I expected him to pull out a vape pen and blow the scent of donuts or banana pudding into the air.

I fist bumped him instead of leaving him hanging, and then turned my attention to the others around us. Would I fight someone from my house or another one? Would it be Lee?

I hoped not. If that was the case, then this whole thing wasn't for me. There was no way in hell I'd go against him. Not because I was scared of him, but because I was scared of what I would do to him. Once I saw red, it was over. I barely remembered half the fights I'd been in, but I damn sure remembered the rush of adrenaline while in the middle of one.

That was what I lived for, and I was counting down the hours—the minutes—until I could feel that sense of liveliness again.

FAITH

Someone bumped into my table as they walked by. I flipped the page in my Moon Phases textbook and took another sip from my coffee without looking up. The dining hall was a madhouse, but I didn't mind. The noise helped me focus. We were only supposed to read chapter five and write a five-hundred-word summary listing three fascinating things we learned from the chapter, but I'd read ahead. I hadn't done my paper yet, but I planned to this afternoon. Once I stopped reading.

Was this how Nora felt when she was reading one of her books?

I couldn't stop. My eyes refused to leave the pages. My finger kept flipping, allowing me to read *just one more page*. The entire concept of our werewolf side being ruled by the moon was fascinating. I had no idea the moon had eight phases, and that each affected our wolf. I'd always thought there were only four—new moon, waxing moon, full moon, and waning moon. I didn't know there were others stacked between that would make certain sensations and feelings of my wolf last longer.

According to the book, during the new moon, our werewolf abilities were easier for us to control. It was easier to shift and easier to maintain control over our wolf. The closer we came to the full moon, the more irritable and unpredictable our wolf was.

It made sense.

I often found my wolf to be more irritable at certain times of the month than others. While I'd never paid much attention to the moon, I would say I'd noticed I had more control over my wolf when we weren't close to a full moon. The closer the full moon was, the more she was in charge of me. She'd always been unpredictable and wild, feral in a sense, but those traits about her came out more when the moon was full than when it wasn't.

My throat pinched tight as a flashback from the night Xavier attacked me shifted through my mind. It had been a full moon. I was glad.

My wolf paced as the memories continued to barrel through my mind. I squeezed my eyes shut and forced my lungs to pull in a deep breath. Time ticked away as the noise of the dining hall grew louder around me. My breathing hitched as the sensation of someone staring at me prickled across my skin. I glanced around, hoping to lock eyes with whoever it was. I needed a place to direct my emotions and anger.

Axel.

He was standing at the entrance of the dining hall with Lee, dressed in dark-washed blue jeans that probably fit his ass like a glove, biker boots, and a plain t-shirt. His tattoos were on display, as were his muscles. He looked mouthwatering. I held his stare longer than I should, but I couldn't help myself. My eyes were drawn to him.

He looked away first when Lee nudged him in the ribs. Lee smiled and waved. I planned on waving back—I started to—but my phone chimed with a new text. My eyes dipped to see who it was from, and suddenly my entire world froze as my heart kick-started it in my chest.

Call me.

Two words. One simple command. That was all it was, but somehow it was enough to make my heart race and my palms sweat.

I stared at my phone, waiting for another message to come through. Nothing else came. There wasn't anything else that needed to be said. What he wanted was direct.

It also scared the shit out of me.

Had he found out something about what I'd done? Did he know why I did it? Was trouble brewing within the nest because of my actions? Was my mother, or someone else, coming for me? Was he?

Shit. Was he here now?

I scanned the faces of those around me. Van being among them somewhere wasn't as unlikely as one would think. It wasn't like this place had security. At least not any I knew of. It would be easy for him to find the place, to find me.

My teeth sank into my bottom lip. It was time I put my big girl panties on and told him at least the barest details of what happened. He wasn't going to go away, and he damn sure wasn't going to let me without any answers.

It had been dumb to even think that was an option.

I gathered my stuff and crammed it into my backpack, deciding now was the time to call him. I was alone. Nora was still at the library, figuring out her newsletter stuff with the librarian, and classes were over for the day. There would be no better time than now. Especially, since I was feeling brave.

"Hey, leaving so soon?" Lee stood behind me. I glanced over my shoulder at him as I zipped my backpack up. There was a tray of food in his hands and a wide smile on his face. "We were going to sit with you."

We? Meaning, he and Axel? Not happening.

My gaze drifted over his shoulder in search of Axel. He stood in line, waiting to pay for his meal. He didn't look my way, but I noticed his back stiffen when my eyes landed on him.

I hoisted my backpack over my shoulder and gripped my cell tight. I grabbed my coffee cup and flashed Lee a small smile. "Sorry. I have to go. You can have my table, though."

Skepticism pooled in his eyes. He was observant; I knew this about him, which meant he most likely knew my smile was fake. I dashed away before he could call me on it, and before Axel reached us. I couldn't afford to get lost in his eyes again, and I damn sure couldn't afford another person seeing right through me. Axel had already done that once, in Strength Training. This time he'd see through my cracks to a place that lived deeper inside me.

He'd be able to see exactly how broken I was, and I couldn't let that happen.

The door to the dining hall flung open before I could push against it, a group of people coming in. I maneuvered around them, not caring when they flashed me nasty looks and scoffed at my rudeness. I dropped my coffee in the trash, and didn't stop walking until I made it to the woods beyond the academy.

Privacy would be needed for this conversation.

I let my backpack fall to the ground as I directed my attention to my cell. My heart rate sped up at the thought of calling Van. Hearing his voice would tear me apart, but it would be his questions and their answers that would gut me completely.

My wolf paced. She was ready to surface, the feel of my fear drawing her out. I licked my lips and pulled in a deep breath. She couldn't handle this for me. Neither could my vampire.

This was all me.

I tapped on the screen of my cell, pulling Van's number up. My thumb hovered over the call button as my heart beat triple time in my chest. When I hit the button, it only rang once before he answered.

"Faith, I'm glad you called." His familiar husky voice made goose bumps prickle across my skin. My eyes closed. How long had it been since I'd last heard his voice? "Tell me your side of the story. Tell me what happened, because my mind has been going crazy with different scenarios as to why you did what you did. I need you to tell me I'm wrong. I need you to tell me that bastard didn't do what I think he did."

The ground, littered with fallen leaves and tiny twigs, swayed beneath my boots. I'd known he would ask. I'd known this was the conversation we would have. What I hadn't been betting on was how much he would seem to care.

"Please. Tell me I'm wrong, Faith," he pressed.

I licked my lips, trying my damnedest to get ahold of myself. Tears burned the corners of my eyes, blurring my vision, but I refused to let them fall.

"Xavier attacked me." My voice shook when I spoke.

I hadn't said the words out loud before. Not to anyone. Not even to myself.

Honestly, I hadn't even put a label on what happened until now. In my head, it had just been something horrible that I refused to think about. But attack, that was the right word. It was the word you used when somebody did something to you that you didn't want.

That you never asked for.

More images from that night broke free from the box I'd shoved them in, and they floated to the surface of my mind. I forced them away like I always did, but the emotions attached to them lingered. Fear crept up my throat. My wolf bristled; her pacing intensified.

He can't hurt you. He can't hurt anyone ever again. You made sure of that.

No. I hadn't made sure of that, but my wolf had.

She'd done what I couldn't. She'd killed him.

"I knew it. I fucking knew it!" The rage in Van's voice startled me. I felt it through the phone. It caressed against my cheek, warming it. I could see his eyes flashing bright with it in my mind. "Why didn't you tell me? Why didn't you tell your mom?"

I'd known this question would come. I'd been expecting it. Still, it sent dread pooling through my middle. "What good would it have done? There wasn't anything anyone could have done for me I didn't do for myself."

Maybe my words were harsh, but they were the truth.

"We could've supported you. We could've been there for you." He let out a sigh, and I knew it wasn't because he was searching for the right words. He was frustrated with me. "I know we aren't together anymore, and I know things with us didn't end on the best of terms, but you know I would've helped you in any way I could. I am now. I know I at least owe you that much after everything."

He did. He owed me that, and so much more, because he hadn't just broken my heart—he'd broken my faith in men.

"What did you do?" I tossed his first text to me back at him. My words were clipped, but it was because I'd already placed my walls back up. That was all the emotion he would get from me. It was all I would show him.

"I knew no matter what happened you did what you did with good reason. I know you. You're not a killer,

Faith. Neither is your wolf. She wouldn't do something like this unless she was protecting you, and I knew you wouldn't set her free on someone like that unless you felt there was a damn good reason."

Van wasn't giving me the answer I was looking for. He was just telling me how well he knew me, which I hated, because if he had known me so damn well, he would have known how in love with him I was.

"What did you do, Van?" I repeated through clenched teeth.

"I sent the nest in a different direction. There's no connection to you. Not even the slightest. I made sure of it. You don't have any reason to worry. No one will come for you. Not over this at least. Your mom is a different story. She might seek you out at some point or another since you've disappeared."

I scoffed because it was highly unlikely she would care enough to search for me. She was probably glad I was gone. Madge Clairemont wasn't the most motherly of mothers. I'd pretty much raised myself.

"You're safe now," he said. I got the impression he wanted me to say thank you, but those words didn't build on the tip of my tongue.

I'd already seen to my safety. Xavier was gone, and I was here. With a new last name. A new number. A new life.

I hadn't needed his help. I'd only needed him to leave me alone.

Silence drifted through the phone between us. I didn't know what else to say.

"Look, I'm sorry," he said after a few more seconds ticked away. "For the way things ended between us. For not being able to love you the way you deserve. And, I'm sorry for what Xavier did." He swallowed hard, the sound of it echoed through the phone. "I can't... I can't even explain how sorry I am for that. I wish it hadn't happened. I wish I'd been there to stop it..."

I couldn't breathe.

A single tear slipped from my right eye. I sank my teeth into my bottom lip, struggling to suppress the ragged breath that wanted to push past them. I didn't want him to hear how much his words had affected me. I wanted him to think they hadn't been enough, because that was exactly how he'd made me feel at the end of our relationship—like I wasn't enough.

The steady drumming of traffic as it rushed down the busy street in the background behind him filtered through the phone. I imagined he was on his balcony, watching from above as strangers passed below.

How many times had I stood there and done the same? How many nights had the sound lulled me to sleep while I lay in his bed?

The silence festered between us. He wanted me to speak. He wanted me to say something—anything—I could feel it. Did he want me to say it wasn't his fault so that whatever guilt eating at him went away? Did he want me to tell him that I wished he'd been there to save me too? Well, he'd better not hold his breath, because it wasn't happening. None of those words would change anything.

Nothing could.

"Faith, I'm sorry," he whispered. His voice cracked, and all I could think was good. "I haven't given your number to anyone else, and I won't. I'll erase it from my phone and I'll protect your privacy. I understand if you want to disappear, but I hope you'll work through this the right way. Mentally. Don't blame yourself for what happened, for what he did, because it wasn't your fault. I hope you know that. I hope you believe it."

"I do." My voice didn't quiver. There was no sob attached to the end of my words. They were firm, strong, because they were the truth. I did know those things. "I promise."

I waited a heartbeat before I hung up. Goodbyes had never been my strong suit, especially not ones with so much emotion attached.

Sobs shook my shoulders less than half a second later. My phone fell from my hand as I broke down. My tears were of relief that everything had been taken care of and that nothing would point back to me, but they were also from what happened and the emotions I still carried. More images of that night shifted through my mind, ripping my insides to shreds and causing more tears to fall. Just because I didn't blame myself for what happened, it didn't mean I was okay with it. It didn't mean that I was past it.

I still hurt. My tears were proof. And, that was okay. I would be okay. In time. I knew this. So did my vampire. So did my wolf, and yet she still itched to be set free, and what she wanted, she got. Especially in moments like this where I felt too weak to fight her.

I kicked off my boots and peeled out of my clothes, tossing them on my backpack as fast as I could. The pulse of shifter magic simmered beneath my skin. My wolf was ready. She was waiting. All I had to do was step aside. So, I did.

Breaking rules had never bothered me. I wasn't afraid of being caught.

My bones stretched and bent. The sensation was familiar. Beautiful. Wanted. I tingled with excitement at not being me for a moment. Life seemed put on pause when I let my wolf take over. I didn't have to feel. I didn't have to think.

All because I was no longer me.

My wolf lunged forward once the shift was complete and barreled through the woods. Daylight still filtered through the branches of the trees and animals scurried around sensing her presence, but she wasn't focused on any of that, all she cared about was running. She needed that release, and frankly, so did I.

AXEL

I undid my tie and then rolled up the sleeves of my uniform shirt as I headed toward the Wolf Blood dormitory. While walking, I passed a few guys with faded bruises across their cheeks or cuts above their brows. We nodded to one another in brief acknowledgement, but didn't speak.

It was all to keep suspicion surrounding the group down.

Fight club had been happening for a few weeks now, and I was feeling saner than ever. My nightmares had subsided. My demons seemed manageable. I was doing well.

I took another puff from my cigarette and felt my fat lip crack open again. The copper taste of my own blood coated my mouth as I snaked my tongue out to lick the area.

Damn, that hurt. Thank goodness it would heal fast.

As I passed Holt Taylor—my first fight and first win—

he nodded and flashed me a crooked grin. He'd been a great contender to go against simply because the rage trapped inside him was his fuel. Fight club was good for him. He needed a way to take out the aggression his human side held tight to from being bitten and turned.

I returned his smile and then cut a left to head inside my dorm house. As always, there were people sprawled around the main lounge, and the vending machines had a line. I started up the stairs, heading for the fourth-floor dorms, not saying much to anyone.

"Hey, man," one of my housemates, Drew, called out as I passed him on the stairs. His dorm was three down from mine and Lee's. "Still down for heading to Last Call for a drink tonight?"

"Absolutely. It's been one hell of a week." No truer words had been spoken.

I was so glad it was finally Friday night. I'd bombed a mixed martial arts test in Strength Training this week because I'd fallen flat on my ass during one of the moves and Professor Blades had failed me. He was a hard-ass. I also had an essay due in Meditation and Spiritual Release I'd worked nearly all week on and almost turned in late despite it. And, there had been a test in another class I wished I'd taken the time to study for.

Yeah, I could really use a drink. Or ten.

"Awesome. See you there," Drew said, continuing down the steps.

I reached the top of the staircase and cut a right toward my dorm. When I reached the door, I unlocked it, expecting to see Lee hunched over his desk nerding out on whatever the hell he'd been researching lately. I was sure it had something to do with Bryant's tattoo. It always did. He'd become obsessed. He'd tried to explain a few more things to me about it, but I'd stopped him. I wasn't here to learn about some stupid secret group he believed was here. He hadn't mentioned it again, but I noticed he'd been more paranoid the last couple of weeks. He'd acted like someone was following him.

Honestly, I was beginning to think he was a bit off his rocker and I was just now noticing.

When I unlocked the door and stepped inside, I was surprised to see the desk chair empty. Lee's bed too. He wasn't here.

"Maybe he finally listened to me," I muttered as I tossed my backpack on my bed and then slipped off my tie. My button-down shirt was next to go, then my slacks.

Where was he? Was he with Nora? If so, I'd let him slide on skipping drinks tonight at Last Call, but if I learned anything different, I'd kick his ass. The guy needed to live a little.

After I changed into my street clothes—which comprised of well-worn jeans, a black cotton t-shirt, and my boots—I shot him a text, asking where he was and reminding him of drinks tonight. He didn't respond. I waited a beat before texting again, letting him know I was heading to Last Call. I pocketed my cell and left our dorm, ready to down a few shots and celebrate making it through another week at Lunar Academy.

* * *

Last Call was a typical small-town bar. I'd come here a few times since being at the academy. It was decent. Cramped, but that was to be expected on a Friday night. There wasn't shit else to do in this town besides come here. Plus, they let those of us from the academy drink regardless of our age. Half the school showed up every weekend because of it.

I snuffed out my cigarette on the bottom of my boot before heading inside. My eyes drifted straight to the bar when I stepped in, pulled there of their own accord, same as always.

She was there, slinging drinks like a pro to two yuppies ogling her.

Faith had a wide smile on her face and seemed in her element. Her hair was pinned up in an intricate bun, and her lips were painted her signature ruby red. She looked good, but damn, I'd been hoping she wouldn't be working tonight. I didn't know why, though; she always worked Friday nights. My gaze remained on her as I stepped farther inside the place. I noticed one of the guys grab her wrist when she slid his drink across the bar top to him, and my wolf bristled. He was always willing and waiting to protect her. So was my vampire, and so was I. She'd wormed her way beneath our skin even more in the last few weeks somehow. I'd tried ignoring her and keeping my distance, but nothing seemed to work. She was always on my mind, always in my thoughts.

She shook the guy's grip off and flashed him a coy smile that sparked a weird, yet strong, sense of jealousy in me. My teeth ground together, my eyes never wavering.

Her gaze met mine as though she could feel me watching her. She kept her expression neutral. Blank. She'd gotten good at putting her walls up whenever I was around. I knew it was because she didn't want me to read her soul any more than I already had.

I understood.

I tore my eyes away from her, and searched for Lync, the other bartender and owner, but didn't see him. Was he in the back? I wove through the crowd of people standing around drinking and chatting, and stepped closer to the bar. I chewed the inside of my cheek while I walked, hoping Lync appeared before I made it so Faith wouldn't have to serve me.

It wasn't that I was opposed to talking to her—hell, there was a large part of me that wanted to do more than just talk to her—it was just best that we kept our distance. She was too much temptation.

My fingers dipped to the ring on my necklace. Ansley flowed through my mind. She was the reason I wouldn't allow myself the comfort of a woman again, because there was always a risk I might hurt them. Even someone like Faith who was of the supernatural world instead of a fragile human like Ansley had been. I had more control over my demons now, but still I worried.

And that worry was enough to make me keep my distance.

My gaze drifted back to Faith. She was serving someone else. I shifted around to scope out the bar, searching for Lee. There was a chance he might have beat me here. He didn't give a shit about changing out of his uniform half the time.

I didn't see him, but I did spot some guys from the dorm house along with their girlfriends. Since Lee wasn't among them, I grabbed my cell from my back pocket and checked to see if there was a text from him yet. Nothing.

Where the hell was he?

"Axel," one guy from our house shouted. "Hurry and grab a drink, then get over here. Alan needs to hear it from somebody else how much of a pro I am when it comes to the roundhouse kick."

I chuckled and gave a nod. The guy landed it twice and now thought of himself as a pro. What the fuck ever. I rolled my eyes as I shifted around to face the bar again.

Faith's eyes were on me—I could feel them—but I didn't meet her stare. Not right away. Instead, I kept my eyes on my cell and waited until she stood in front of me.

"Hey, is your roommate here?" she asked in her husky tone.

Damn, I loved her voice.

"He's supposed to be, but I don't think he'll show." It was a feeling I had in my gut.

I'd pushed him too hard on coming out with me tonight, so he'd probably holed himself up in the library. I just hoped Nora was there with him.

Faith placed a hand on her hip. Irritation prickled off her. It was cute. "Great. He was supposed to have a book for me. One I need to help write my paper for Moon Phases. I was supposed to get it from him in essentials, but he never showed."

My brows pinched together. "He never showed?"

Lee always went to class. I'd never even heard him tease about skipping before.

"Nope. And, I need that book. My paper is due Monday."

"Monday, huh? Procrastinate much?" I grinned. She didn't think it was funny.

"Whatever." She rolled her eyes as she reached for a rag to wipe down the bar top with. "Whenever you see him, let him know I really need that book." Her eyes flashed when she spoke.

"Will do, but I think he's with your roommate right now, so I might not be seeing him tonight at all."

She narrowed her eyes. "He's not with Nora. She's in a meeting for that library newsletter thing of hers. I just talked to her about thirty minutes ago."

Okay, if he wasn't with her. Or in our room. Or here. Where the hell was he?

Something wasn't right.

"You sure about that?" I asked.

"Yeah." She scoffed as though she couldn't believe I had the audacity to question her on it.

"Give me your phone." I held my hand out.

"Excuse me?"

"Your phone. Give it to me," I insisted. "Lee wasn't in our room. I waited around for a while, so we could come here to meet the guys together, but he never showed. I texted him, but he didn't answer. And, now you're telling me he missed class. That doesn't sound right. I'm going to head back to our dorm to see if he's there. I want you to text me if he shows up here."

She blinked. "Oh. Okay. Sure."

She passed me her phone, and I input my number before pressing send to make a call. My cell rang, and I saved her number. "There. Now, like I said, if he comes in after I leave, send me a text and let me know."

I handed her cell back to her. Her face broke into a wide smile when she took it. "This is a joke, right? Some warped way to get my number?"

I pushed myself away from the bar and stood. "If I wanted your number, I'd straight up ask. I'm not the type who enjoys playing games." My words weren't harsh; they were honest. From the look in her eyes, she seemed offended, though. Maybe I'd made it sound as though I wasn't interested in her with what I'd said, which couldn't be further from the truth, but she didn't need to know that. I'd let her think what she wanted. I had other things to worry about—like where Lee was.

How was it possible he'd skipped a class? Essentials for him was before lunch. Had he gone to any classes before that?

I hustled to the exit, ignoring Alan and the others asking where the hell I was going. I didn't have time to fill them in. My gut told me something was wrong.

When I made it back to the dorms, I bolted up the stairs toward the fourth floor and then dashed down the hall to our room. I swung the door open to find it still empty. Lee wasn't here. My eyes snapped to the area beside the desk where he usually kept his backpack—it was empty. He hadn't been here. Shit. I grabbed my cell and instead of shooting him another text, I called. It rang until his voicemail came on. I hung up. My gaze darted around the room. It was then I noticed his comic book collection was missing from the shelves above the desk.

What the hell?

I stepped farther into the room and noticed the desk was clean. Too clean. Nothing was on it. Nothing was in it. The shelves above were bare. I bolted across the room to Lee's dresser. When I opened the top drawer, it was empty. So were all the others. I stepped to the closet. His clothes were gone.

My head cocked to the side as I backed away from the closet. What the hell was going on? Where were Lee's things? Where was Lee? Had his stuff been here when I left to go to the bar earlier? Or had he packed up in the last thirty minutes and left? Left to where?

The room spun. My gut twisted. There was something wrong.

I swung the door to the dorm open and slammed it shut behind me before stalking down the hall to our advisor's dorm. Pete would know what was going on. He'd be able to tell me where Lee was.

My mind raced as I walked. Had he swapped for a new roommate? I thought we'd gotten along good, but maybe I'd been wrong.

I knocked on Pete's door, hoping he was home and not out celebrating making it through another week here like I should be. Like Lee should be with me. When no one came to the door right away, I knocked again.

"Yeah?" Pete shouted through the door before he swung it open. He sounded irked, but when he saw me, his back straightened and his pissed off expression melted away. He folded his arms over his chest and glared at me. I knew he was trying to make himself seem intimidating, but I wasn't about to call him on it. All I wanted to know was if he knew where Lee was. "What's up?"

"Lee. My roommate. Where the fuck did he go?" The words grounded out with more force behind them than necessary, but I was having a hard time controlling my demons with my head being such a mess.

Something passed through Pete's eyes, but it was gone before I could name it. His hands dropped to his sides. "You didn't know he planned on dropping out, I take it."

I blinked. Dropping out? Lee? Not a chance in hell. He'd never drop out. "He wouldn't do that. He loves this place."

Pete shrugged. "Sorry, man. I don't know what to tell you."

"No, I'm not buying it." I shook my head. "He didn't even tell me he was having problems."

"Sometimes they don't. Sometimes they just dip out without a word." Pete slapped me on the shoulder. "Most of the time, the roommate misses the signs. There are always signs though. Always."

My chest tightened. I couldn't imagine Lee doing that. He would have said something to me if he was having problems, wouldn't he? My mind raced. Were there signs I'd missed? "Did he swing by here before he left?"

"Yeah."

"What did he say? What reason did he give for leaving?"

"Oh, I didn't see him. When I came back from my last class, the dropout form was shoved beneath my door." He scratched his neck. "Most who drop out don't see me face-to-face to do it. I think it's because they worry I'll try to talk them out of leaving."

"Did you go to our room to try to talk some sense into him?" I asked, unbelieving it could be that easy to leave a place like this.

Pete shook his head. "Nah. Dropouts are common. Some can't handle the rules. Some can't handle being around other werewolves. Some can't handle the classes. Everyone has their reason, and it's not my business as to what that reason is. We're all adults here. If someone wants to leave, I let them."

My fist clenched at my side. I'd really thought Lee and I were closer than that. If he'd been thinking of leaving, he would have said something to me. At least, I thought he would.

I guess I was wrong.

"Look, I understand you thought the two of you were friends, that he wouldn't have left without saying something to you, but he did. Everyone always thinks that whenever their roommate dips out. The problem is, they don't say shit to anyone because they're afraid to admit they can't handle it here. I've seen it half a dozen times. Don't take it personally."

I wanted to tell him he didn't know what the hell he was talking about, that he didn't know Lee, but instead I clamped my mouth shut and headed back to my dorm. Once inside, I closed the door firmly behind me and pulled out my cell to call him again. Just like before, it rang until it went to his voicemail.

Damn it.

Without thinking through what I was doing, I pulled up Faith's number and called her. It rang four times before she answered, the noise of the bar filtering through the phone.

"Hey, Axel," she said. "I wasn't expecting you to call me so soon."

"Is Lee there?"

Please let him be there, drinking a beer and laughing with the guys.

"Nope. Haven't seen him. I messaged Nora to see if he was in the library, but she checked and he's not there either. Everything okay?"

"No." I closed my eyes and smoothed a hand over my face as a sigh escaped me. "What time do you get off?"

"Now that's a line I've heard before." Amusement hung in her tone.

"It's not a line. My gut is telling me something's off about all this. I need someone who knows him to help me find him."

"Eleven," she said, all the amusement gone from her tone. "I get off at eleven."

"See you then." I hung up. I didn't know if pulling her into this was the right thing to do—hell, I didn't even know what I was pulling her into—but my gut was telling me something had happened to Lee.

Things weren't adding up.

My gaze drifted around the room again, seeing if there was anything I'd missed. Something in the closet caught my eye, causing my gut to twist.

The comic card in the plastic frame he was obsessed with. It was still there.

FAITH

I popped the lid off my latte, so it could cool after situating myself across from Axel. We sat in awkward silence, him refusing to even look at me. I could tell it was because there was a lot on his mind. He looked distraught. Worried. The area between his brows was pinched tight, and he chewed the inside of his cheek. I tried not to stare, but it was hard not to.

His tongue snaked out to moisten his lips, and I felt the area between my thighs warm. He chose that moment to look up. His eyes locked with mine, and I wondered if he knew where my thoughts had dipped. Could he sense it? My arousal?

"So," I said, feeling unease twist in the pit of my stomach. "What do you think happened to Lee? You said you have a bad feeling?"

"I can't explain it." His eyes darkened. "Something isn't right about the whole thing."

"What thing?" I didn't understand what he was getting at.

"Lee didn't just skip class. Apparently, he dropped out."

I blinked. "What? There's no way he would do that." I knew I didn't know Lee super well, but I knew him well enough to know he wouldn't do something like that. Not without a serious reason behind it. "Is his stuff gone? How do you know he dropped out?"

"Yeah, it's gone. I also talked to Pete, our advisor, and he said Lee turned in the dropout form to him."

I shook my head, sending a few stray hairs free from my updo. No wonder Axel looked so distraught; this was crazy. "That can't be right. Lee wouldn't have just dropped out like that. He wouldn't have done it without saying something to someone." I locked eyes with Axel. "Did he say anything to you about leaving?"

"No. That's why this isn't making sense. I'm assuming he didn't mention anything to you either, right?"

"Not at all."

I leaned back in my seat and reached for my latte to take a sip. My mind flashed through the last couple of weeks, searching for any sign Lee had been thinking of dropping out. Nothing came to mind. There had been cuts and bruises on Lee from time to time, though.

The Viking-looking guy with the scar.

The few times I'd seen Lee with him, he always seemed tense and uneasy. Could he have been the reason Lee left the academy?

"Was he having problems with someone?" I asked, wondering if Lee had mentioned the guy to Axel.

"No, why?"

"Because I think he may have been bullied."

Axel grinned. It was a sexy lopsided grin that did things to me, which seemed inappropriate for the situation we were in. "Why do you think that?"

He was his roommate, hadn't he seen the cuts and bruises on Lee? Although, hadn't I saw them on him too? Were they beating each other up? Why didn't I press Lee for answers about where they'd come from?

"I noticed Lee had bruises and cuts a few times over the past few weeks. A couple times he even came to class holding his ribs like he'd broken something. Every time I asked him about it, he always said he couldn't talk about it." I watched Axel, trying to judge his reaction. He was hard to read, though. "I'm thinking someone was bullying him. The question is, who?"

"He wasn't being bullied."

"How can you be so sure? I remember this muscular guy with a scar who looks like a Viking, that Lee always seemed uneasy and tense around, talking to him a few times."

"That would be Bryant. He wasn't bullying Lee." Axel's tone was so confident it irked me.

"You didn't see the exchanges between them like I did. Lee seemed freaked out by him."

Axel took a sip from his coffee. It was black. No cream. No sugar. I shivered as I thought about how bitter it would taste. "It's not what you're thinking. Bryant wasn't bullying Lee. Their exchanges were all part of something else."

"Like what?" I narrowed my eyes on him.

"I can't say."

I pushed away from the table and folded my arms over my chest. If he wanted me to help him find Lee, then he needed to give me all the details. "You asked me here because you're worried about him. You think something bad might have happened. Yet, I'm here telling you things that might equate to a possible cause for his disappearance, and you're nearly laughing at me while withholding information. How the hell are we supposed to work together on this if you're not telling me everything?"

"Point made." Axel nodded. "All right, I'll tell you, but you can't tell anyone else. This has to stay between us."

I took a sip of my latte, my eyes never wavering from his. "Fine."

"There's an underground fight club here that Lee and I are a part of. Bryant too. He runs the thing, actually. That's why you saw Lee and him talking. It's also why you saw the bruises and cuts on his face from time to time. Mine too."

I broke out into laughter that I couldn't contain. "You really expect me to believe that? Lee was too nerdy to be in something like that. I can't even imagine him volunteering for it. There's no way he'd have taken part in it of his own accord."

"Well believe it, because he did. He was pretty damn good at it too. It's the quiet guys you have to watch out for. Most of the time they have a lot of pent-up anger inside."

I searched his face for any sign he was teasing, but there was none. Axel was serious. There was an underground fight club at Lunar Academy, and he and Lee were a part of it.

What. The. Hell.

I leaned forward, placing my palms on the table between us. "You're serious?"

"As a heart attack, darlin'."

"First off, don't call me darlin'. I don't do pet names. Second, how did I not know something like that existed here? Are females not allowed?"

"Actually, there are a few. Bryant doesn't allow them to fight with men, but they sure are kicking each other's asses twice a week."

My skin prickled with excitement. So did my wolf.

"Again, how the hell did I not know something like this existed?"

"It's invite only, and we keep it under wraps." He shrugged.

Okay, so apparently, I wasn't cool enough to be on the invite list. Whatever.

"So, if he wasn't being bullied, then what was going on? We both agree that we don't think Lee would've up and left without saying anything. What do you think happened?"

"I'm not sure." He scratched at his neck. "I don't know where we go from here either."

"How about we head back to your place and search

for clues," I suggested, not thinking through the way it sounded.

Axel's eyes twinkled with amusement. "Is that a line?"

"I don't need lines."

"Touché." He chuckled. He took another sip from his black coffee and then leveled his eyes with mine. His face turned serious again, and I knew that our teasing moment was over. "I did look around while I was in the dorm last. All of his stuff was gone except for his favorite comic card he always kept in a case. He used to get onto me about slamming our dorm room door too hard and knocking it over. It was his prized possession, and I know there's no way he would've left it behind. That's what really has my gut twisting about this situation."

A lump formed in my throat. Had someone' else packed up Lee's things and accidently left that behind, not knowing how much it meant to him?

My stomach flipped.

I popped the lid for my latte back on and pushed my chair out to stand. "Let's see if there's anything you might have missed."

"Sounds like a plan." Axel grabbed his coffee and stood as well. "And, thanks for agreeing to help me work through this."

I glanced at him. "No problem. Lee is my friend, too."

"I know. That's one of the reasons I sought you out."

We exited the coffee shop near Last Call without another word and headed back in the direction of Lunar Academy.

It was about a twenty-minute walk before we were back on campus. We headed straight for the Wolf Blood dormitory and climbed the stairs. When we reached the fourth floor, I followed Axel down the hall to his room. It was past the co-ed curfew, but everyone who looked our way didn't seem to care. They flashed us a knowing smirk that suggested we were off to do something we weren't, and my insides fluttered. I hadn't thought about how it would look—me going into Axel's room so late in the evening. This was exactly how rumors got started, but there was nothing I could do about it now. We'd already been spotted.

Besides, I wanted to scope out Lee's side of the dorm and see if anything else had been forgotten or a clue had been left behind.

Axel opened the door to his room and then motioned for me to step inside first. As I did, his cologne filled my nose. It did things to me that I tried my damnedest to ignore. He closed the door behind us, and I forced my eyes to glance around the room. It was clear which side was Axel's. The bed was unmade, and his uniform lay on the floor. A few personal items could be spotted here and there, but nothing major like posters or pictures. I turned my attention to Lee's side of the room and noticed it was bare.

"I see what you mean. It looks like everything of his was wiped out." I stepped farther into the room. "Did you already look through his drawers and stuff?"

"Sort of. I went through everything pretty quick. There didn't seem to be anything left behind, though."

I still checked for myself. Once I saw they were empty, I headed to the closet. The comic card Axel mentioned was on the shelf. I recognized the guy on it. Lee had a few t-shirts of him too.

"There's nothing else here," Axel insisted. "This just doesn't make any sense."

"Well, what do we know to be true?" I asked. "The paperwork says Lee dropped out. His stuff is gone to back that up, but he forgot to take his most prized possession with him. Was he in a hurry to leave, or did someone else pack his things for him? Did someone do something to him, and this is their way to cover it up?" The thought crashed over me like ice water.

Shit. Was that what happened here?

"I'm not sure. I don't know why he would have been in such a hurry to leave, but I also don't know why someone would pack his stuff for him to cover anything up. I mean, this is Lee we're talking about. He's a nice guy. I can't think of a single soul who didn't like him or would want to hurt him."

"I know."

I glanced around again, searching for anything we might have missed.

"The only thing I can think of that it might be in relation to is something he was sort of obsessed with lately," Axel said.

I paused in rifling through the desk drawers to look at him. "What's that?"

"A tattoo. It was related to some story his crazy uncle told him a few times while growing up. Something about a secret group. I never allowed him to elaborate because conspiracy theories aren't my thing."

"A tattoo and a secret group?"

"Lee spotted the tattoo on Bryant the first time we met him. He freaked when he saw it, and I guess he never let it go. He just kept digging."

"And the tattoo was linked to the secret group?"

"I think so. Like I said, I didn't pay attention when he talked about it. It all seemed like nonsense to me."

"So, you don't know what the tattoo stood for, or remember anything more about the group?" I asked.

"No. I wish I did, though. All I know is he thought the tattooed symbol on Bryant stood for the group, like a branding."

I arched a brow. "If Lee was right, I bet Bryant isn't the only person at the academy involved with the group. What if they found out Lee was researching them and kidnapped him to keep him from digging too deep?"

My chest tightened. I didn't want that to be the case, but it was the best motive we had at the moment.

"Anything is possible," Axel said.

Something on the floor beneath the desk caught my eye. I crossed the room and bent to retrieve it. It was a scrap of notebook paper.

"What's that?" Axel asked. He stepped closer and glanced over my shoulder to read it.

It was a list of names. I didn't recognize any of them except for Bryant. His name was underlined as well as four others, the rest had question marks beside them.

"Pete. He's our advisor." Axel pointed to one of the names.

"Do you think he was hiding information from you earlier?" I asked. "Did you happen to see the form Lee supposedly filled out?"

Axel's jaw tensed. "No."

Could their advisor have been the one to cover up Lee's disappearance by making it look as though he'd dropped out? If that was the case, who the hell was this group, and why did they feel so threatened by Lee of all people?

AXEL

I stormed out of the dorm and headed straight for Pete's. My fists were clenched at my sides as I walked, and my teeth ground together. All I could think about was how that fucker had lied to my face.

He knew where Lee was; I was sure of it now.

Faith followed me without a word. No lights were on when we reached Pete's dorm. I pounded my fist against his door, not caring if he was asleep.

"Think he's here?" Faith asked. She stood close, too close. I could smell her sweet scent—coconut and vanilla. "He could be out partying still. It's barely after midnight."

My lips pressed together as I knocked again. Nothing. He wasn't home. Shit. I glanced at Faith. "Down for a little B and E?"

Her eyes flashed. Something about it had me thinking this wasn't the first time she'd been involved in a breaking and entering. While this surprised me, it also excited me. I loved a girl with a hellraiser inside her.

"If it helps us figure out what happened to Lee." She pulled a bobby pin from her hair and stepped forward to tinker with the door. Seconds later, it swung open. She motioned for me to step inside first. "After you." Her ruby red lips twisted into a beautiful grin.

I slipped into the room. "Damn. I'm impressed. I'm also guessing this isn't your first offense?"

She closed the door behind her, and then pulled out her cell to use its flashlight. I did the same. "Nope."

I waited for her to elaborate, but she didn't. The conversation fizzled out as we glanced around Pete's room. It was the same size as mine; the only difference was he had the place to himself. There was a single bed. A dresser. A desk with a chair. And, a TV. I swung the flashlight of my cell around, searching for anything that might lead me to Lee. I realized two things about Pete quickly. One, he was a complete slob. And two, he really had a thing for cheese puffs. There were empty bags all over the room.

"This place is gross," Faith said. She picked through the mess of stuff piled high on his desk. "How does he find anything in all of this?"

"It is pretty disgusting in here." I made my way to his closet. There wasn't much inside besides a couple of academy uniforms and standard street clothes.

Time ticked on. And, we found nothing. Irritation prickled through me.

"Wait a minute," Faith suddenly said, drawing my

attention to her. "Do you have that piece of paper with the names we found?"

I reached into my back pocket for it and handed it to her. "Why?"

"I think I remember this name." She took the paper from me and compared it to the one she'd found on Pete's desk. "Miranda Ridge. I knew the first name looked familiar."

I leaned over her shoulder, trying to ignore the coconut vanilla scent floating off her skin that made her smell good enough to eat. The note was written in a female's handwriting.

Meet me at the usual spot. 10 a.m. Bring the snoop.
Miranda

"Looks like Pete had a meeting with her. With as messy as he is, this had to have been from today. It would have been buried already if not." Faith moved around a cheese puff bag with disgust. "I'm guessing the snoop was Lee, and that Pete dropped him off to her."

It was a good theory. I just hoped we weren't reaching too far. If this was all panning out the way my gut was telling me, I didn't think we had much time left to find Lee before something even more awful happened to him.

"So then, I think our next move would be to track down Miranda." Faith locked eyes with me. "She might be more helpful than Pete. I mean, this place is a mess and I don't think we're going to find anything else besides this here." She waved the scrap of paper.

I opened my mouth to agree with her, but a knock on Pete's door had the words dying in the back of my throat. I switched off my flashlight. Faith did the same. We froze in the center of the room, hoping whoever was on the other side of the door realized Pete wasn't home and left.

"Pete?" a guy called out. "Hey, man. You in? I got that guy's name you were askin' for."

I locked eyes with Faith. It was clear from her expression she was thinking the same thing I was—maybe it was the name of someone else this secret group was getting ready to abduct.

A piece of paper slid under the door. Faith and I remained where we were, standing so close to one another in the dark that I could feel her breath tickling my neck and her body heat pressing against me.

Footsteps sounded in the hall. The guy at the door had left. I put distance between me and Faith as I made my way to the paper he'd left on the floor. I picked it up and switched my flashlight on again to read it. The name was for a guy on our hall I'd met a time or two. He was in my Meditation and Spiritual Release class. The dude was built more like me than Lee, so any theory this group was looking for a specific type of guy was out the damn window with that.

Faith came up beside me and glanced at the paper. A few strands of hair fell from her updo to tickle my forearm. "Hey, I know that guy. He's in my Moon Phases class. We have the same lunch too."

"I know him too."

She took a step back, and I was thankful. That slight amount of distance allowed me to keep control over myself while still in a dark room with her. It had been a long time since I'd had such a physical reaction to a woman before. It was overwhelming.

"What's the connection between Lee and him? There has to be something," she said. "Why else would the same group want them both?"

I scratched my jaw. "I can't think of anything other than they're both from Wolf Blood. Maybe it's something to do with our house?"

"Like what, they're weeding us out?"

I set the piece of paper back on the floor in front of the door. "I don't know, but it seems likely."

Faith placed her hands on her hips. "I'm not sure where we go from here, but first things first, we need to get out of here before Pete comes back."

I checked my cell. It was after one now. We'd been in this mess of a room for over an hour.

"Let's go, then."

"Where to?"

"Back to my room. We can figure out our next step there," I suggested.

Faith nodded and pocketed her cell before reaching for the door. She locked it from the inside and then stepped through. I followed and then closed the door behind me. The hall was empty and for that I was thankful. We didn't need anyone seeing us sneaking out of Pete's room. Not if he was up to what we thought he was—abducting members of our house for whatever reason.

It would put us on his radar, and I didn't think that was a safe place to be.

When we reached my dorm, I flipped on the lights and took note to how eerily quiet it was now that Lee wasn't here.

I missed the guy.

Lee was the first friend I'd made in years. I didn't get close to people anymore, but somehow, he'd wormed his way in. I hadn't realized how deep until now.

"Out of these names, we're certain Peter and Miranda have something to do with Lee's disappearance and possibly whatever secret group is lurking around the academy," Faith said. "We think Bryant might be part of the situation thanks to his tattoo, and we think this might have something to do with just our house. Do you know if Pete has the same tattoo?" Her eyes locked with mine.

"I'm not sure."

"That's something we might want to check out. Noting the tattoo on others might tell us how big this group is we're dealing with."

"Right, so basically we don't know shit about what happened to Lee."

She folded her arms over her chest. "Pretty much."

The two of us fell into silence. Minutes ticked away before Faith broke it.

"I say we follow Miranda tomorrow and see what we can learn about her. We need to look for that tattoo. If she has the same one as Bryant, then we know they're both involved with the same group and that it's the group who took Lee. Hopefully, we'll be able to figure something else out that might lead us to where he is."

It was a big hope, but I didn't say so.

"I'll touch base with Pete again. He plays basketball with some others on the courts during lunch. There's a chance he might show more skin there."

"Planning on checking him out? You interested in him?" she teased.

I stepped closer to her—so close our breaths mingled in the air between us. "While I have no issue with the LGBTQ community, I can tell you that Pete isn't my type." I tucked a strand of loose hair behind her ear and leaned in. "You are, though."

Faith shivered. Her tongue slipped out to moisten her perfect lips, and it took everything I had not to lean in and kiss her.

What the hell had I been thinking saying that? What had I been thinking when I stepped so close to her?

All I could smell was her heavenly scent. All I could feel was the erratic pounding of my heart inside my chest and the desire to kiss her—to taste her—throbbing through me. Her pupils dilated, and I knew she felt it too.

The air between us sizzled with our chemistry.

I inhaled. The scent of her arousal heightened my own. My eyes locked with hers and her breath hitched. A cocky grin sprang onto my face. She knew what was coming, and she wasn't pulling back. I dipped my head closer, erasing a fraction of the remaining space between us, my eyes never wavering from hers. Her head tipped up to allow me easier access to her mouth, and her eyes closed. I marveled at the way her dark lashes fanned against her creamy cheeks.

She was gorgeous.

My hands gripped her hips. I pulled her closer until she was pressed flush against me. Her scent filled my nostrils, and I felt both my demons go crazy because of it. Control wasn't something I had anymore. My lips crushed against hers. The taste of her lips spurred a divine hunger inside me I didn't know waited there. I wanted more of her—I wanted all of her—the need was so overwhelming it nearly brought me to my damn knees. She grazed her teeth over my lower lip, and I thought I was a goner.

My fingers traveled up her back until they reached the base of her neck. I tilted her head to the side, exposing it for me. Damn, I wanted to sink my teeth into her—to explore all the pleasures and pain we could bring one another—but I refrained. Instead, I sucked on the tender skin there and listened to her moan.

It was a sound I'd been dying to hear for weeks.

I inched her toward my bed. She collapsed across it when the backs of her knees hit the mattress. I eased on top of her, ready to take this as far as she was willing. My hand slipped beneath her shirt, feeling her smooth skin against my heated palm. She withered beneath me, placing her center against my throbbing member. The friction nearly sent me over the edge. It had been too long since I'd been with a woman. I knew I wouldn't last long because of it.

Faith pulled at my clothes. Each article she tugged off me, I did the same to her. In seconds, we were skin to skin across my bed. Nothing had felt this right to me in forever.

Her nails dug into my back as she bucked her hips, letting me know what she wanted to happen next. I obliged, lining myself up with her slick center. One thrust, and I was in. She moaned as my hips moved in a rhythmic pace until both our worlds shattered apart only to fuse back together again.

Bliss was the only word to describe it.

FAITH

I sat in the dining hall at one of the café-style tables, waiting for Axel. We were supposed to meet at four. I checked the time on my cell. It was seven minutes past. He was late. Worry festered in the pit of my stomach. Had something happened while he'd been scoping out Pete in search of whatever crazy tattoo this group shared, or was he ghosting me after last night?

It wouldn't be the first time. Van had been notorious for it. Somehow, being ghosted by Axel seemed as though it would hurt more though. I'd thought there had been a connection between us last night, one that ran deeper than any I'd felt with Van.

I gripped my cappuccino too tight as my teeth worked over my bottom lip. My eyes remained glued to the entrance of the dining hall, watching for Axel while my mind continued to circle through my worries.

Minutes later, he finally showed. My shoulders relaxed as relief trickled through me. I took a sip from my cappuccino and allowed my eyes to trail over him. Underneath his eyes was dark, and his lips were pressed into a thin line. A fresh bruise had formed across the bridge of his nose.

My back straightened. What happened? Had Pete and him fought?

While I knew Axel could handle himself—he was part of an underground fight club after all—I still worried.

"Hey," I said when he was closer. "You don't look so hot. I'm guessing it didn't go well with Pete."

Axel's lips twisted into a crooked smile as he situated himself in the chair across from me. Now that he was closer, I noticed his bottom lip was swollen. "As well as expected. Pete was playing basketball like I figured he would be, but apparently, wolves don't play typical ball. They play street ball, but with absolutely no fucking rules." His grin grew, and I watched as his tongue snaked out to lick along his bottom lip. It was sexy as hell and had me thinking of the things he'd done with his mouth last night. "Wish I'd known that sooner. I enjoyed myself."

"I'm sure you did." I chuckled.

"What's this? You bought me a coffee?" He picked up the cup and took a sip. "Black. Just the way I like it."

"Yeah, I remembered from last night."

A subtle sense of emotion shifted across his face, dulling his grin and darkening his eyes. His fingertips reached for the ring that dangled from the chain around his neck. I'd noticed it before. He seemed to touch it from time to time.

I took a sip of my cappuccino, hoping to wash away questions about the ring building on the tip of my tongue. It didn't work. As soon as I swallowed, they flew from my mouth.

"What's that about? The ring on your necklace?" I pointed to it. "I noticed you wear it every day."

Axel released his hold on the ring. It fell to his chest and glistened in the crappy lighting of the dining hall. "It's a reminder of my biggest mistake."

His words were soft, yet raw. They held the power to break me.

My mind dipped to places it shouldn't, forming questions that would do me no good to ask because it was clear from the hard set of his jaw that whatever his mistake was, it wasn't something he was willing to talk about.

Still, I wondered. Whose ring had it been? A lover? A fiancée? A wife?

Jealousy prickled up my spine.

I forced my mind to clear and placed all my walls back up. Whoever his past lovers were, and whoever that ring belonged to, was none of my concern. We'd slept together last night. While I wanted it to mean something, I wasn't going to fool myself into believing that it did. We'd both been worked up over the craziness surrounding Lee. He was where my head needed to be, nowhere else.

I opened my mouth to steer us back to talk of Lee and ask if Axel had noticed a tattoo on Pete, but Axel had other plans.

"The ring belonged to Ansley. She was going to be my fiancée. This was her promise ring," he said as he lifted the chain so I could see the delicate silver ring with a tiny green jewel better. "I wear it to remind me of her. To remind me of why I'm here at Lunar Academy—to learn control."

I licked my lips. "I'm sorry." I hadn't expected him to tell me something so personal, but I was glad he had. It made me feel more confident in the connection I felt budding between us. It made it more real.

"Don't say you're sorry. Her being gone isn't your fault. It's mine."

I wanted to press for more details, but I didn't because I feared he would put his walls back up. He seemed like the type to shut down easily. I could tell because I was too. "I know. I'm just sorry because I misjudged you."

"People often do." He dropped the ring and took another sip from his coffee.

I cracked a grin. "Yeah, well you remind me a lot of someone else. I can see now I was right in my comparisons in some ways, but not all. You definitely have someone from your past who still haunts you exactly like he did." I left off the part about it meaning that he wasn't available for anyone in the future because of it. That was something I was secretly hoping to be wrong about.

"Is this the guy who upset you not long ago? The one who called or texted with something you didn't like?"

My stomach tightened. I hadn't thought he noticed me so much.

"Yeah, that's exactly who I'm talking about. My ex." I ripped my eyes from his and took a tentative sip from my cappuccino. As far as I was concerned, this conversation was over. I wasn't going into all the juicy details of Van and why we'd broken up. I didn't want to talk about how much more I had loved him than he'd loved me. And I damn sure didn't want to talk about what his text messages were regarding. "We should probably get back to talking about Lee. Did you learn anything from playing basketball with Pete? Does he have the same tattoo that Bryant does?"

"Yeah. He does."

My heart skipped a beat inside my chest. I wanted to think of Lunar Academy as a safe place where we could learn more about our nature, but it appeared there was something—or someone—sinister lurking on the grounds.

"It's on his chest instead of on his hand like Bryant's," Axel insisted.

"Oh, that's not good." I swallowed hard. "The tattoo could be on any part of their bodies, then. It could be completely hidden beneath their clothes. We'll never know how many of this group there are because of it." I shifted around in my seat as my wolf immediately became on edge.

I pulled in a deep breath, trying to calm her. The last thing I needed was for her to take charge of the situation and cause me to shift in front of everyone.

Unpredictable, she was.

"I know. Did you have any luck with Miranda?"

"No," I grumbled. "She worked all day at the flower

shop in town. She doesn't seem like the type to be a part of some secret organization. She's pretty boring. Actually, she reminds me a lot of Nora." At the mention of Nora, I remembered that Miranda actually worked on the library newsletter with her. "Speaking of, Nora mentioned Miranda's name this morning. She's part of the library newsletter thing Nora works on too. Apparently, they're supposed to go over some graphics together today. I told her to text when Miranda gets to the library."

"Does she know why you want her to text you?"

"No. She didn't press for details."

"What are you planning on doing once she lets you know she's there? Head to the library and stare at her?"

"While pretending to read a book." I smiled, and he chuckled. My cell chimed with a new text. I glanced at the screen. "And there's my roomie now. Looks like Miranda just showed up. I'd better get going." I gathered my things to leave.

"When should we check back in again? I'm thinking about heading back to the basketball courts to see if Pete is still there. I might follow him around some more and see if I can learn anything else."

I glanced at my cell, checking the time. "It's a quarter till five now, so how about we touch base at seven?"

"Sounds like a plan." He picked up his coffee and nodded toward me in agreement.

I stood still for a heartbeat longer than I probably should, simply because I wasn't exactly sure what we were supposed to do when parting—shake hands, hug, kiss? I mean, we had slept together.

"Okay." I tucked a few strands of hair behind my ear. "Well, I guess I'll touch base with you at seven, then. Good luck." I started to walk away, but he grabbed hold of my wrist, forcing me to pause.

"About last night," he said, his voice low. Goose bumps prickled across my skin as I stared into his heated eyes. "It meant something to me, and I just thought you should know."

A smile worked its way onto my face. "It meant something to me, too."

"I'm not sure if this, whatever it is, is something either of us is ready for," he insisted as he worked his fingers between mine. "But, I'd be lying if I said I didn't want to see where it leads."

I swallowed hard. "Me too."

His thumb moved in slow circles along the back of my hand as we held one another's stare. My heart thumped hard in my chest. This wasn't something I'd been expecting from him. Heck, neither was what happened last night.

Another text came through on my cell. I was sure it was Nora, since I hadn't responded to her yet. I'd been too focused on the awkwardness rushing through my veins at the sight of Axel, and trying to figure out what our next move in finding Lee should be.

"I should probably go," I said without releasing his hand. "There's no telling how long Miranda will be in the library, and I'd like to see if she has a visible tattoo."

"Yeah. Okay, so we're meeting back up at seven?" He released my hand and stood.

"Meeting up? Sure." I'd thought we would just call or text to fill one another in. He was serious when he said he wanted to see where this went between us. Cool. "Where do you want to meet?"

"Do you like Mexican food?"

I arched a brow. "Who doesn't?"

"I feel the same way." He chuckled. "How about we meet at Nachos?"

I tried not to swoon at the thought of their cheese dip. The place was one of the few restaurants in Brentwood I had saved in my phone. They weren't too far from the bar, so it was fast and easy to place a pick-up order before my shift. I wouldn't admit to how many times I did that in a given week.

"Sure. I love their quesadillas." I hoped my face didn't light up as much as it felt like it did when I said that.

"I haven't had them yet. All I've had is their cheese steak tacos." He took a sip from his coffee before placing a hand against the small of my back and heading toward the double doors of the dining hall. My wolf came to the surface at the feel of his touch. I think she liked him. "All right, then it's settled. We'll meet at Nachos at seven."

"See you soon." I'd almost said it was a date.

Was it a date? We had both said we wanted to see where this thing between us went.

"Be careful with Miranda," he whispered as we paused in front of the dining hall. "If she truly is part of this group, then you should keep in mind she might be dangerous."

Miranda worked with flowers four hours a day and was part of the library newsletter. I was positive I could handle her just fine but didn't say so.

"I will," I said instead. "You should do the same with Pete."

"I will." Axel leaned in and pressed his lips against mine.

They were warm and gentle, yet somehow held fire. His teeth skimmed at my bottom lip, and I melted against him. Someone whistled, causing the kiss to end too soon, and I glanced at the jerk responsible.

"Nice," he shouted. "How about one for me?"

A witty response built on the tip of my tongue, but Axel let out a low growl that scared the guy away faster than anything I could have said.

Damn, he was sexy.

AXEL

I finished the rest of my coffee as I headed back to the basketball courts. It was closer to five now and dark clouds were rolling in. This didn't seem to stop those still playing on the court. In fact, they seemed to enjoy themselves even more. Maybe it was because along with the dark clouds rolling in, a breeze had kicked up as well.

"Back so soon?" Ryan Grayson, a guy from my essentials class asked with a grin when he spotted me. He was from Wolf Born and always seemed to have a chip on his shoulder because of it. Still, the guy was decent.

"Yeah, I guess so. Needed a refreshment and something to eat. You guys are hardcore out here." I peeled off my shirt and tossed it on the bench like I had earlier. "If I'd known, I wouldn't have waited so damn long to play."

"Shooting hoops is one of the best ways to get out some of that pent-up aggression from not being able to shift whenever the hell we want. That's one of the rules I hate most about this place. That and the damn uniforms."

"Couldn't agree more," I said.

My gaze drifted around the court. There were only four baskets, and since there were so many of us playing at once, that meant there were four half-court games happening at one time. Each game had one basket. Pete had been playing at this one before I left, but now I didn't see him.

Where had he gone? Was he done for the day?

It was possible. He'd already been out here for a few hours. Maybe I should have just sent Faith a text letting her know I spotted the tattoo but wanted to stick with Pete so I could continue to monitor him instead of meeting her for coffee in the dining hall. While it would've been logical, it would've made me look like an ass after last night.

Faith deserved better than that.

"Think fast, Stone!" Ryan shouted before launching a basketball at me.

I caught it in midair and dribbled toward the basket, ready to perform a layup. A few guys let out a round of applause as the ball swooshed into the net. To my right, I caught sight of Pete at the next court over.

He stood to the side, chugging from a water bottle. I kept an eye on him as the boys lined up to let me dunk the ball again. He seemed to be taking a break, but he also seemed to be texting heavily with someone. I wondered who.

Miranda? Whoever had Lee?

The desire to jerk his cell from his hand pulsed through me, but I knew I had to refrain. Doing so would only open a can of worms I wasn't sure we were ready for, and it would no doubt create a fight on the court that would have multiple guys jumping in. Everyone here had adrenaline rushing through their system, causing their wolves to remain just below the surface.

I remained where I was, focusing on both the game and Pete. When my cell chimed with a new text, I reached for it, having a feeling it would be Faith with news.

"I'm taking a timeout for a second," I called to the guys. "Let Steve take my spot." I nodded to the guy on the bench nearest our basket. He was a short guy with a blond mohawk and loads of anger issues. The two of us were cool though. We'd fought one another a couple weeks ago during fight club and gained respect for each other because of it.

I'd won, of course, but Steve had given me a run for my money.

I reached for my cell, but before I glanced at the screen, I felt someone's eyes on me. I looked up and found Pete staring at me. His eyes were dark and intense as they roamed over my face. Something about his stare caused my demons to stir. My teeth ground together as I fought to remain in control. Steve slapped me on the back as he passed behind me, causing me to tear my eyes from Pete.

"Thanks, man," Steve said.

"No problem."

When I glanced back at Pete, he was gone.

I jogged to the bench and grabbed my t-shirt. My gaze swung around as I searched for him. I spotted him. He was almost to the faculty and staff building.

What was he going there for?

It was Saturday. I assumed all the teachers and staff were off campus doing whatever they did on their days off.

As I followed him, I glanced at my cell. I'd been right —Faith had been the one to text me.

Done here. Graphics didn't take long to approve, apparently. I think she knows I'm following her too. She looked at me funny.

I glanced up to look at Pete, just as he slipped into the faculty and staff building. My gut told me he knew I was following him too.

Looks like both of us have been found out. Pete's going into the faculty and staff building. I'm following. You be careful. Touch base with me soon to let me know you're okay.

I jogged toward the building, not wanting to let Pete get too big of a head start on me. However, if he knew I was following him, he was probably waiting inside for me.

You be careful too. I'll check in with you in about thirty minutes. Nora is with me now. She refused to let me out of her sight until I filled her in on what's going on.

I hated that she'd brought someone else into the fold

with us, but I understood. Nora was too close to Faith to not be suspicious of things. Plus, she was probably already wondering where the hell Lee was. The two of them had seemed to hit it off and then he'd disappeared.

I pocketed my cell and pulled in a deep breath to center myself. With my fist clenched tight, I opened the door and slipped inside. The building was as fancy as any other on campus. It was built of stone and resembled something out of the medieval ages while also somehow seeming modern. My sneakers squeaked against the polished tile floors as I moved deeper into the building. The place seemed empty. Dead. However, I could hear hushed voices coming from one of the rooms nearby.

One voice was male and the other female.

I was too far away to distinguish if the male was Pete. Plus, there seemed to be a strange grinding noise muffling their voices.

What the hell was that?

I inched my way down the hall, trying to figure out where the voices were coming from. They disappeared before I could pinpoint them, and I was left standing at the base of a staircase that led up to the second floor of the building.

Where had Pete gone? He practically disappeared.

I made my way back down the hallway, peeking into the open rooms and pausing outside the ones with closed doors, listening for him. There was no way he could've went up the stairs. I would've heard his footsteps echoing back to me. He had to have gone into one of the rooms, but it seemed as though all of them were empty.

What the hell?

I stepped into the main lounge, thinking maybe he'd went into the back section where all the vending machines were. It was empty. Just like the rest of the room. The same grinding sound from earlier floated to my ears again, and I paused, holding my breath so I could pinpoint where it came from.

"You need to see Fletcher," a female voice snapped. "If your fears are as you suspect, you should not have come to me. You should have gone directly to Fletcher. Either him or Carver. Do not come to me again. Do I make myself clear?"

I had no idea who Fletcher or Carver were, but I knew one thing—whoever this woman was, she was pissed.

"Yes, ma'am."

Pete. That had been Pete talking. So, he was here after all. Where the hell had he been hiding?

"You are dismissed," the woman insisted before the sound of heels clicking against the tile floors echoed through the hall. Thank goodness she was heading in the opposite direction, because there was no way in hell I wanted to be spotted by her. She was obviously pissed to have had her weekend disturbed by a student.

Pete let out a breath before the sound of his sneakers beating against the tiled floor heading in the opposite direction from where I stood floated to my ears. I peeked out of the lounge to see where he was headed. He stepped all the way to the end of the hall and opened the door with a plaque on it that read *Boiler Room*.

Why the fuck would he go down there? Was Fletcher a maintenance man? What about Carver? Did Lunar Academy even have maintenance men or janitors? Honestly, I hadn't seen a single one since arriving on campus. I imagined everything was cleaned with magic.

I waited a few beats before I opened the door to the boiler room and followed Pete, wanting to make sure he would be down the stairs and chatting with whoever he was hoping to find. The stairway was dimly lit, and I noticed right away that the air down here was thicker than it had been on the other side of the steel door. Had this room been a dungeon at one point? My mind wandered through the possibilities of what I'd find at the base of the stairs as I descended them. My demons surfaced, both itching to take full control of the situation and shove my humanity to the side.

Darkness surrounded me as soon as I reached the bottom of the stairs. It didn't bother me. What bothered me was the silence. If Pete was down here along with someone else, they should be making noise. They should be talking. There should be a light on somewhere.

"Damn it. I knew you were fucking following me," Pete growled from somewhere behind me.

I spun around to face him and came in contact with something metal. It smashed against the side of my head, causing a blinding pain to ripple through me and darkness to pull me under.

FAITH

I had my eyes locked on Miranda as she speed-walked toward the Wolf Bound dormitory. She was one of us—a Wolf Blood—so why was she heading to our rival house's dorms? Something wasn't right. I could feel it in my gut, and whatever it was, it had my wolf pacing.

Nora huffed beside me as we continued to follow Miranda, being sure to keep a good distance. "I still can't believe this. I mean, it's like something from one of the books I read."

Nora hadn't shut up since I'd filled her in. I knew I would regret bringing her in the loop on things. Still, I'd done it anyway because I liked her. We'd become friends over the last few months. This was something too big for me to leave her out of any longer. Besides, I knew she wouldn't believe Lee had dropped out any more than Axel and I had.

I'd been right.

"It's crazy to think she's part of some secret group on campus. Do you think there's only one? Or is there another?" Nora grabbed my wrist and inhaled a sharp breath. "There's probably a rival group. There always is. Good versus evil."

I didn't let my mind wander too far down that rabbit hole. If I did, I knew I'd become paranoid and my wolf might take over. She liked to come out to play when I was in emotional distress. I was getting better at controlling her, and steadying my emotions, but I still had my moments now and then.

"Which do you think Miranda is part of—the good group or the evil one?" Nora asked in a whisper. She'd let go of my wrist when we stepped around a cluster of girls blocking the sidewalk. "I can't even believe she's part of a group at all. She's so quiet. And nice."

Miranda slipped behind the Wolf Bound dormitory and disappeared. My wolf bristled. I understood. Not having her in sight any longer meant there was a chance she'd grabbed the upper hand and could be waiting to attack on the other side of the building.

She had given me a suspicious look at the library. I thought I'd been careful at the flower shop, but maybe I hadn't been careful enough. Could she have spotted me there too? If so, then she would definitely be waiting on the other side of the building for us.

Shit.

I forced Nora to a standstill. "We need to come in from the opposite side. I think she'll be expecting us to follow her this way."

"Right. Okay." Nora's face scrunched up. "Maybe we should split up. You go one way, and I'll go the other." She reached out for my wrist again. "No. Wait a minute. Then she would just attack one of us. It would be a minute or two before the other could help."

I loved that she'd finished her thought before I could tell her how bad an idea splitting up was. "Exactly. Let's just stick to going in the opposite direction she did. Together."

Nora nodded and then linked her arm through mine. We crossed in front of the Wolf Bound dormitory, both of us keeping our eyes peeled for Miranda in case she was close by watching and waiting. I couldn't sense anyone's eyes on us. It didn't mean there wasn't anyone watching us, though.

Adrenaline spiked through my system.

When we reached the opposite side of the building, I drew in a breath and unlinked my arm from Nora's, preparing to fight should the need arise. My wolf snapped at me. She wanted me to set her free. My vampire strength rushed through me at the same time. While I knew neither side of myself would put me at an advantage against Miranda, considering she was from the same house as I was, I was still glad both sides of me were just as ready as the other in case she attacked.

I glanced at Nora. Her fists were in front of her, ready to swing should Miranda be waiting. The two of us stepped around the building at the same time. I wasn't sure what I expected to see, but an empty space wasn't it.

Miranda wasn't back here.

"Where did she go?" Nora whispered.

I glanced around. "I'm not sure. Maybe in through the back door?"

I wasn't sure if that was where she'd went, but I figured it was possible. We inched closer to the French doors off the back of the dormitory. If the building was anything like Wolf Blood's, then those doors led to the main lounge. While I didn't understand why Miranda might use the back door instead of the front door, I didn't discredit the possibility.

"What should we say if someone asks what we're doing here?" Nora glanced at me. Anxiety rippled off her in waves, causing my wolf to feel even more uneasy about this entire situation.

"We'll think of something if it comes to it." I had no freaking clue what excuse would make us look the least suspicious. And really, it all depended on how confrontational the person who spotted us happened to be.

I peeked through the glass doors to the main lounge. There were people sitting on the couches, a couple of guys at the pool table mid-game, and a girl in the recliner. There wasn't any sign of Miranda, though.

Where the hell had she gone?

I stepped away from the doors when I noticed the girl sitting cross-legged on the recliner with her laptop looking at me.

"Okay, she's definitely not in there," I said. I grabbed Nora's arm and steered her away from the doors.

"Where could she have gone, then? We weren't too far behind her. She didn't have that much of a head start.

If she ran in there, someone would have stopped her to ask what she was doing. It's not even her dorm house."

"My thoughts exactly." I glanced around the grassy area behind the dormitory. There were no greenhouse buildings or maintenance sheds out here. It was a patch of grass and then the start of the woods a little distance away. There was no place for her to go besides inside the dorm house. Unless... "What if she went into the woods?"

Nora glanced in that direction. "It's possible."

I scanned the woods as well. There was no sign of Miranda, but that didn't mean she hadn't darted to them when disappearing behind the building and worked her way deep inside.

I started for them. Nora followed. When we reached the edge of the woods, I stepped through. Nora grabbed my wrist.

"Wait a minute, are we going in there to look for her?" she asked.

"I think this is where she went. To do what, I don't know. But my guess is, it has something to do with Lee and the secret group. Are you coming?"

Nora released her grip on me and glanced at her feet, causing my eyes to dip there. She wiggled her toes in her pair of thin flip-flops. "I'm not dressed for hiking in the woods. Plus, I'm allergic to poison ivy."

"Are you serious?" What wolf is allergic to poison ivy? Typical human afflictions didn't affect us.

Well, this was true most of the time.

There was a guy in my essentials class—a Wolf Blood —who was allergic to garlic. His revelation of that had everyone laughing, including the professor, since it's nothing but an old vampire myth.

"It's embarrassing, but yeah. For whatever reason, when I'm in my human form I'm allergic to poison ivy, sumac, and oak. It's something I learned the hard way. Trust me." Nora scratched her arms as though just the thought of it irritated her skin. "When I'm in wolf form, I'm fine, though. I can roll in it and not have an issue."

"So, maybe you should shift." I arched a brow and flashed her a grin. She didn't seem to think the suggestion was funny.

"And break a rule? No, thanks."

"Are you sure? It would kill two birds with one stone —you wouldn't get poison anything and you'd probably be able to catch a whiff of Miranda's scent. Then we'd know for sure if she came into the woods, and if she's in here alone."

The thought of someone else being with her sent a shiver up my spine.

"It's broad daylight. I'd totally be caught," Nora insisted.

"Okay, then just wait here. I'll be back in a second."

"I don't think it's safe for you to go in there alone. I don't think Miranda is a giant threat—she seems like too sweet of a person—but one of the things we both know about the supernatural world is that looks can be deceiving." She carefully stepped over some low-lying brush and made her way into the woods. "I'll just watch my step."

"Okay, but I still think shifting is a better idea."

"Why don't you do it, then?"

"Because, I'm not the one worried about getting an itchy rash." It wasn't even close to the truth.

The truth was, I was afraid to shift and allow my wolf control. I didn't know if I'd be able to rein her back in. My adrenaline was high, and my wolf was too uneasy in this situation.

It was best if I remained in human form and kept control.

As Nora and I walked deeper into the woods, neither of us spoke. There didn't seem to be any sign of Miranda, but there was a whiff of something unfamiliar lingering in the air here. Nora locked eyes with me the instant she sensed it too.

"Magic?" I whispered.

"Yeah, but Wolf Bounds aren't supposed to use magic outside of the classroom. It's a rule."

A rule that didn't matter to someone.

If Miranda was with whoever it was, I didn't think we'd find her anytime soon. While I didn't know exactly what type of magic hung in the air here, I knew I didn't want to be a part of it. Not with Lee's disappearance and some secret organization on campus.

"Let's get out of here," I suggested as I turned back.

Nora didn't argue. Instead, she headed back the way we came without a word. Soon we were back to the edge of the woods near the Wolf Bound dormitory making our way around to the front of the building. When we reached the sidewalk, I pulled out my cell and shot off a text to Axel.

I lost Miranda. Something strange is going on in the woods behind the Wolf Bound dormitory. I think she's working with someone who's using magic beyond the classroom.

Nora picked up her pace, leaving me behind. I glanced behind us, thinking someone was following us but didn't see anyone suspicious.

"What's wrong?" I asked as my wolf bristled.

She made a face. "I have to pee so freaking bad. All this excitement has my last bottle of water rushing right through me."

I laughed. And then pulled out my cell again to send another text to Axel.

How are things going with Pete? Any luck on finding out anything else?

When he didn't respond right away, I shoved my cell into my back pocket and tried to keep up with Nora as we speed-walked back to the Wolf Blood dorms. The girl was fast when she had to pee.

AXEL

*M*y head hurt like hell. Dots speckled the edges of my vision as I swung my head from left to right.

Where was I?

The place was dimly lit and hot as a fucking sauna. It smelled like sweat and something else. What was that? Air freshener? Had someone recently sprayed something to try to cover up the stench of the place? There was something else—another scent mixed in—but I couldn't name it.

The hair on the back of my neck lifted as two sets of eyes settled on me. Wherever I was, I wasn't alone.

A chair scraped against the concrete floor, catching my attention. I spun to my left to see who I was dealing with and felt a sharp pain shoot through the side of my face.

Why was I in so much pain? What the hell had happened?

An old fire extinguisher a few feet away caught my eye. That was the source of my pain. I knew it. Pete had hit me with a damn fire extinguisher. My demons fumed. I lifted a hand to rub against my throbbing face, but soon realized I couldn't. My hands had been tied together—my feet too—with rope. Magical rope. That was the other scent I'd noticed. Magic.

Shit. This wasn't good.

"Do you know how much trouble you've caused by following me?" Pete snarled from somewhere behind me. Like I'd sensed before, he wasn't alone. There was someone else with him. I could feel their eyes on me.

Someone stepped from the shadows in front of me. It took me a second, but I recognized him. He'd sat in on a couple of my classes. He wasn't a professor, but more of a teacher's assistant. He wasn't assigned to any professor in particular. Instead, he seemed to bounce around doing whatever the professors needed him to do.

He was their bitch. Plain and simple.

"Don't come at him just yet," the T.A. insisted. He held up a hand to Pete. "Let's see what he knows first."

He stepped closer and narrowed his eyes. I knew he was waiting for me to spill my guts to him, but there was nothing to spill. I didn't know shit about what I'd stepped in. The only thing I knew was that they had Lee.

I glanced around, trying to figure out where I was. Was this still the boiler room? It had to be. There were pipes and steam... and a fancy wooden desk? What the hell? That seemed out of place.

"He knows more than he should. That's the problem," Pete insisted. I shot him a look from over my shoulder, regretting the quick movement as soon as the white-hot pain stabbed through the side of my head. Pete moved to sit on the edge of the desk.

Was this the T.A.'s office? What was his name? Wasn't it Fletcher?

I'd never had any run-ins with him, but I knew Lee had a time or two. They nerded out over something together a while back. My mind drew a blank on what it had been. I blamed the hard hit to the head with a fire extinguisher. I glared at Pete. What an asshole he turned out to be.

"Well, come on, then. Tell me what you know. Tell me why you were snooping around," Fletcher pressed. He paced in front of me with his hands clasped behind his back. "What about Pete is it that interests you so much you'd follow him down here?"

"I don't give a rat's ass about Pete," I spat.

Pete slammed his hand down on the desk, drawing my attention to him. "You were looking for your nerdy friend, weren't you?"

His sneakers squeaked across the concrete floor as he moved to stand. He walked toward me. When he reached me, he gripped my shoulders tight and jerked me around, twisting my lower back at an odd angle.

"Well, you found him. Bravo," Pete growled as my gaze landed on Lee.

He was on a cot in the back corner of the room. His eyes were closed, but I could tell he was still breathing.

He was okay, just sleeping. Or maybe he'd been knocked out like I had been.

"What made you go searching for him?" Fletcher asked. He'd come to a standstill in front of me. "You two didn't even seem to have anything in common."

"What do you want with him? Why take him?" I asked, ignoring his question and instead asking my own.

"You can't answer a question with a question, but I'll let it slip this once." Fletcher tsked. He glared at me over his pointed nose. The dude had witch-like features. "Your friend was looking into things he shouldn't. Same as you. Haven't you ever heard the saying curiosity killed the cat? Well, in this case it just might kill the wolf."

My cell chimed with a text. I knew it was Faith. Shit. I didn't want them to connect the two of us. I didn't want her in danger.

What if she already was, though?

"He was digging too deep, so you tried to erase him. Well, good luck trying to erase me too." They were bold words, but they were the truth.

How many students could they take and use the ruse of them dropping out before someone caught on? Things would look suspicious if they tried to do the same to me too, especially since Lee and I were roommates.

Fletcher paced again. I glanced at Pete. He moved to lean against the desk again, chewing on his thumbnail.

"He's right," Pete insisted. "We can't do the same thing we did for Lee to hide his disappearance. It'll look too suspicious. You know who will get onto us then. You know how things have to be for—"

"Don't say another word! We don't know how this will pan out, which means we don't need him learning anything about what we're involved in from either of us," Fletcher was quick to say.

My mind circled back to what Pete had been about to say—was he going to say he or she? Not that it would matter much whether the person in charge of this group was male or female, but it could be a good piece of information into helping solve this puzzle.

Was it the woman I'd heard him talking to before?

My cell chimed with another text, the sound of it seemed to spark anxiety in both Fletcher and Pete. While the two of them went back and forth over what they should do next, I worked at the knots on the magical rope holding me in place. Whoever had tied them didn't know the trick behind them. It wasn't long before I was free. When that happened, I wasted no time attacking Pete first. He was closer. One knee to the stomach and a double-fisted crack to the back of the head and he went down. I lunged for Fletcher next. He tried to reason with me, but I wasn't listening. One right hook and he crumbled to the ground, out cold.

My feet pivoted, and I lunged in Lee's direction. The ache in my head intensified, but I ignored it. I nudged Lee when I reached him, trying to wake him, but it didn't do any good. He was sound asleep. A bottle of water on Fletcher's desk caught my eye. I grabbed it and twisted the cap off before splashing it on Lee. He bolted into a sitting position and smoothed his hands over his face.

"What the hell, dude?" he shouted.

Relief trickled through me at the sound of his voice. He was okay. "I had to get you up somehow." I shrugged. "Come on. We need to get out of here."

"Where are we?" Lee glanced around.

"The boiler room. You got yourself in some serious shit digging around."

His eyes bulged. "What? Digging around what?"

I headed toward the exit. Was he serious? Had they done something to his mind? "Um, the tattoo you were so freaked about ring any bells? The secret group you mentioned, maybe? They came after you, man. They kidnapped you."

His jumped off the cot and was at my side in an instant. "You're joking, right?"

"No. I wish I was."

His hands smoothed over his face. "Oh, shit!"

"Yeah. I came home to our room empty of your stuff and Pete telling me you'd dropped out." I grabbed the metal knob on the steel door to the boiler room. It was cool to the touch as I twisted to swing it open.

"No way."

I glanced both ways, making sure the coast was clear before stepping into the hall. "Dude, I seriously couldn't make this shit up if I tried. Thank goodness I didn't buy into it."

Lee ran his fingers through his hair as he followed me through the exit. Before long, we were standing in front of the building, making our way down the sidewalk. We garnered some attention thanks to our speed-walking, but we needed to get the fuck out of here before Fletcher and Pete woke.

"How did you know?" Lee asked as we maneuvered through a group of people on the sidewalk.

I glanced at him and flashed a smile. "They left your prized possession behind. It's still in the closet. Still in its plastic case. Plus, Faith found a piece of paper with some names of people you'd been checking out it seemed."

"Faith?" Lee arched a brow as a goofy grin spread across his face.

At the thought of her, I reached for my cell in my back pocket. We were supposed to have checked in by now with each other. I imagined the text messages that came through before I took out Pete and Fletcher were from her. I hoped nothing had happened to her.

"Yeah, Faith. And, we're not talking about her right now. We need to figure out what our next move is, because they'll come for us as soon as they wake up."

I glanced at my cell. The text messages had been from her. There were three. The final one asked where I was and said she'd be waiting in the dining hall at the same table we were at earlier. Nora was with her.

"We have to get out of here, then. We need to pack our shit and go. This group is serious, Axel," Lee shouted. "I still don't know exactly what they're up to, but I'm positive it's not something I want to be involved in."

"Shh, keep it down. We have to get Faith and Nora first. They're in the dining hall. I can't leave them behind. They're as much involved in this as I am."

As soon as we entered the student center, I made my

way back to the dining hall and spotted Faith and Nora at our table. Faith noticed us first. Her eyes widened when she spotted Lee.

"Oh my God, where have you been?" she asked once we were closer.

"Apparently, I've been holed up inside the boiler room for who knows how long." Lee grimaced.

"We can't stay here, and it's damn sure not safe to talk here. Come on." I nodded toward the doors before starting that way again.

"Where are we going?" Lee asked. "They'll be looking for us. Soon."

"I know. The first place they'll look will be our room, so we need to get there fast and get our things. Then we'll head to the girls' room and get the hell out of there."

"According to you, they already took my stuff. What am I supposed to do?" Lee asked.

"I don't know, but I need to grab some of my stuff."

"Maybe we should split up. Then we can meet somewhere. It'll be faster," Faith suggested.

I glanced at her. "No. We stick together. They're dangerous."

I refused to argue with her on this. Plus, I didn't want her out of my sight. Neither did my demons. I had to make sure she stayed safe.

When we reached our dorm, I used my ID card to let us in. I took one step into the room and froze. All of Lee's belongings were back where they had been.

"What the hell?" I muttered as I stepped farther into the room.

Lee scratched his head. "Uh, I thought you said my stuff was gone."

"It was," Faith said. "I saw it."

"Then, how did it get back so fast?" Lee asked.

"No, the question is why," Nora insisted as she closed the door behind her. "They wouldn't have gone through the trouble to bringing your stuff back—which had to have been done by magic, since the scent is still in the air —unless they were planning on letting you stay, right?"

My stomach twisted. Were they planning on getting rid of me, then? My gaze drifted to my side of the room. Everything was still there. "Apparently, they aren't planning on getting rid of me either. I don't understand."

"Neither do I," Nora insisted.

"Do you remember anything?" Faith asked Lee. "Did you overhear anything, or figure out anything more about them? If you didn't, maybe they decided you weren't as big a threat as they originally thought."

"Still, they wouldn't let us go," I insisted as I reached for my duffel bag from inside the closet and began shoving clothes inside. "We all know too much now."

"Not really," Lee insisted. "I mean, I figured out my uncle was right about the secret group existing. I recognized the tattoo, exactly like I've been saying. I also know there are a few others on campus that are being recruited. Or at least I think they are. Ryan Grayson is one of them. Him and this girl I have a class with, Nadia Hazel, they came to me about a week ago, maybe two, asking if I knew anything about the group. Apparently, word got around that I was obsessing over something having to do with a tattoo and a group. That's why I think they came for me. I was drawing too much attention to them. I think my meeting with Ryan and Nadia was the last straw. I'm not saying they tipped off the group, but I am saying I was being watched exactly like I thought, and when they saw them come to see me, they didn't waste much time after before they came for me themselves."

"If that's all you know, then Faith might be right," Nora insisted. "Especially since we don't know anything more than you. Maybe they figured that out somehow."

"I'm not taking any chances," I insisted as I moved to my dresser and begin cleaning it out. "You three shouldn't either."

"I know the group has something to do with humans," Lee said, ignoring me.

They all seemed to be ignoring me when I claimed we still needed to get the hell out of here.

"Something to do with humans?" Nora repeated.

"Yeah, I wouldn't say this group is anti-human, but I do think they feel superior."

"Superior to humans?" I asked Lee as I shoved my last pair of boxers into my duffel bag while glancing at him.

"Maybe. Probably." Lee scratched his head. "I didn't get to look too much deeper because they nabbed me. The last thing I remember was Pete and this girl named Miranda from our house knocking on our door. After that, all I remember is waking up to Axel pouring water on my face."

"Yeah, still not sorry about that. I had to get you up somehow, like I said."

"Yeah, yeah. Whatever," Lee grumbled.

I opened my mouth to say something else, but a knock at the door had my lips clamping shut. My heart sped up.

"Shit. We're out of time," Lee insisted.

I put my finger to my lips and set my duffel bag down. "You two get in the closet." I pointed to Faith and Nora.

"Not a chance. If you're going to fight them, so are we," Faith insisted. She folded her arms over her chest and dug her heels into the floor.

She was stubborn as hell. It was one quality about her I loved.

"Fine. Brace yourself for a fight, then, because I'm not going down easy." I flashed them a grin and popped my knuckles before reaching to open the door.

I expected to see Pete or Fletcher on the other side, but instead there was a girl. She had long dark hair with purple tips and brown eyes. She wasn't familiar to me, but I could tell right away she was from Wolf Bound.

"Can I help you?" I asked.

She opened her mouth, and I thought she was going to say something, but instead she lifted a closed fist to her mouth, splayed her fingers open, and blew on green dust resting in the palm of her hand. Before I could move out of the way, it worked its way into my nostrils and then seeped into every pore as it suffocated all of us standing inside the dorm.

A dark haze slipped over my vision as the girl stepped into the room and closed the door behind her. I fell to my knees, choking on the dust. My gaze sought out Faith. She was on the floor too, choking like me. My wolf howled as my vampire fought his way to the surface. It did no good though; whatever she blew in my face had stripped away my mobility. I was frozen, falling prey to the dark haze sweeping over my eyes and pulling me down into blackness.

I locked eyes with Faith. She was scared. So was I, but I was also pissed. How could I have pulled her into this with me? What the hell had I been thinking?

History was repeating, and again all I could do was watch it unfold, unable to stop it.

The girl with the dark hair spoke. Not to any of us, but to someone on her phone.

"It's done," she said in a low tone. "They won't remember a thing to do with the Elite now."

FAITH

I grabbed my purse and jacket from the back room before reaching for my timecard, ready to clock out.

"Where do you think you're going?" Lync asked.

"I asked three nights ago if I could leave early tonight. Axel and I are meeting with some friends at Nachos," I said. Was he shitting me? I'd said this to him multiple times, so he wouldn't forget. Lync always seemed so lost in his head.

He flashed me a grin. "Chill. I'm just kidding. I remember. I'm not that old and senile yet."

I rolled my eyes. Old and senile? The guy was barely twenty-five.

"Have fun. Are you going to the end-of-semester dance tomorrow?"

I arched a brow. "How do you even know about that?"

He didn't go to Lunar Academy. He never had,

because he couldn't. He was human. At least I thought he was.

"I hear things. Especially since you college kids are my best customers." He winked.

"Keeping tabs on academy parties. That's not creepy," I deadpanned.

"Whatever. Get out of here." He chuckled. "Your boyfriend is waiting at the door. Tell him I said if he doesn't quit standing there looking so hateful, I'm going to have to hire him as a bouncer, so he doesn't make this place look so rough and tough, and scare my clientele away. That way he'd at least make them feel safe."

I glanced at Axel. He was propped against the wall near the entrance, dressed in his leather jacket and a pair of worn blue jeans. He had his biker-looking boots on too. My heart fluttered, because damn he looked good.

"I'll tell him he needs to at least come sit at the bar when he's waiting on me instead of standing at the door," I said as I waved to Axel before heading in his direction.

"I'm kidding. Don't tell him that. I don't need him coming after me."

I flashed Lync a grin. "Fine, have a good rest of the night. I'll see you on Tuesday."

Thank goodness this place was closed on Sundays and Mondays. It gave me a three-day weekend where I didn't have to work or go to classes. I loved it.

Especially now that I spent every second I could of my weekends with Axel.

"Yep, see you Tuesday," Lync called after me.

When I reached Axel, I stood on the tips of my toes

and gave him a kiss before pulling on my coat. "Hey. You're here early."

"Only because I'm starving. I was hoping Lync might let you off early if he saw me over here." He flashed me a wicked grin.

"Yeah, about that. He said you need to stop doing that because he's afraid you'll scare away his customers. You might have to be hired as a bouncer if you plan on standing there while I work."

"I don't know about that. Working at a bar isn't my thing. Drinking at one is." He dropped his arm over my shoulders and steered me out of the bar. "Let's get out of here."

"Think Nora and Lee are already there?"

"Oh, yeah."

"Good. I hope they got us a table in the back."

"I'm sure they did."

I didn't mention that I'd sent Nora a text asking that she please get us a table in the back because I knew how much Axel liked sitting there. I also knew how much my next words would freak him out. "So, about tomorrow night... I decided I want to go to the end-of-season dance."

He glared at me. "You can't be serious."

"I am." Not really, but I wanted to see him squirm. "I didn't go to the last one, and I heard a few of the upper-class girls chatting about how this one is always the prettiest. Supposedly, there are white lights and ice sculptures. It's a winter wonderland theme. Might be fun." I shrugged a shoulder to keep my joke going and glanced up at him. His face had paled. Dances weren't his thing. He'd said so more than once over the last couple days.

"If you want to go, I guess we can." He scratched his neck.

"I'm joking. I seriously have no intention of going." I laughed. "Just wanted to see you sweat."

He growled and then tickled me as we entered Nachos. I laughed and wiggled away from him, but it did no good. He still came after me.

"Look at the two of you, acting all happy and shit," Lee said as he eyed us with a wide grin.

"Seriously, what's gotten into you guys?" Nora asked. "You're both always so moody looking."

Axel pulled the chair out opposite Nora and motioned for me to sit. "This one decided she would pull my leg about the dance and make me think she wanted to go." His eyes looked menacing, but the curve of a smile twisting at his lips softened them, making him look sexy as hell.

"I really had him going. He was sweating hardcore," I teased him as I sat.

"I don't know about the sweating part, but she did have me going." Axel situated himself beside me. "Anyway, did y'all order yet?"

"Just drinks," Lee answered.

"And cheese dip. Large, of course," Nora added with a smile.

"Of course," I agreed. No one came to Nachos and didn't get cheese dip. It was legendary.

Someone bumped my chair. "Oh, sorry. These tables are tight in here."

I glanced up and saw a girl I remembered from around campus.

"Miranda, hey," Nora greeted her with a smile. "Did you get those new banners I sent you this morning?"

"Yeah, I loved the blue one. It really makes the book you reviewed pop." She tossed a smile back to Nora and then pulled out her cell. "I was thinking of tweaking this one though. Here's what I came up with. Sorry, I forgot to email you back." She leaned over and flashed Nora her phone. When she did, I noticed a tiny black tattoo behind her ear.

"Cool tattoo," I said.

Her fingers lifted to touch it. "Thanks."

"Tattoo?" Lee asked. "Can I see?"

Miranda looked to the guy she was with, and I swore hesitation flitted through her eyes. Or was that panic? "Yeah. Sure. It's nothing really." She shifted so Lee could see.

"Nice," Lee said with a nod.

"Yeah, I like what you did with the color scheme. We should totally use your banner instead of the other one," Nora said.

"Thanks. I think so too." Miranda pocketed her cell. "Well, have a good night."

"You too," Nora said.

Miranda and the guy she was with walked away, just as our waiter came with Lee and Nora's drinks. Once he left with mine and Axel's order, Lee shifted his attention to Axel.

"Wasn't that Pete with her?" he asked.

"Yeah. Guess that's the girl he's been making moan like a porn star on a nightly basis."

I slapped Axel's shoulder. "Ew. Gross."

"Seriously," Nora chimed in, backing me up as the guys laughed. Her attention then shifted to Lee. "And why did you want to check out her tattoo? You've never cared about tattoos before." Irritation rippled through her words.

Lee shrugged. "I don't know. I've been thinking of getting one lately."

"You want a tattoo?" Axel asked as he leaned his elbows on the table. "Since when?"

"Since the last fight when I beat that guy's ass." He took a sip of his soda and gave us all a look that said he was still super proud of himself for his takedown.

"The guy was like four inches shorter than you and twenty pounds," I said, remembering how Axel had described him.

"So, I still took him down."

I cracked a grin. He was right. I saw the guy the next day in the student center. He'd had a nasty black eye. Apparently, one punch had been all it took.

"So, what are you thinking of getting?" I asked Lee.

He smoothed along his jaw. "I'm not sure. I'm thinking—"

"I swear, if you say the name of one of your stupid comic characters I'll hurt you," Axel insisted.

"That was my first thought, but now I think I want like a boxing glove or something that represents fighting."

The sensation of someone staring at the four of us prickled across my skin. When I glanced up, I spotted Miranda and Pete standing at the cash register. They were still waiting to pay, but their eyes were fixed on us. Miranda smiled and then both of them looked away. Unease twisted in my gut and my wolf bristled. There was something about the two she didn't like.

The waiter came with our drinks then. When I glanced back at the register, Miranda and Pete were gone. Nora said something, and my attention shifted back to my friends and my boyfriend as I shoved whatever it was I felt toward Miranda and Pete from my mind. They didn't matter. What did, was this new family I'd created for myself at Lunar Academy.

THANK YOU

Thank you for reading *Wolf Blood*. We hope you enjoyed it! Please consider leaving an honest review at your point of purchase. Reviews help us in so many ways!

Stay up to date with the authors:

Visit Alyssa at https://www.alyssaroseivy.com
Stay up to date on Alyssa's new releases: ARI New Release Newsletter.

To see a complete list of Alyssa's books, please visit: http://www.alyssaroseivy.com/book-list-faq/

Visit Jennifer at https://jennifersnyderbooks.com
Stay up to date on Jennifer's new releases: Jennifer's Newsletter
To see a complete list of Jennifer's books

please visit: https://jennifersnyderbooks.com/book-list/

The Lunar Academy will continue with Wolf Bound, Year One coming in October!

Eager to find out more? The Lunar Academy continues in *Wolf Bound*, book three in year one. New house. New couple. New clue to the mystery.

Four Houses. Traditions. Secrets. And Romance Waiting At Every Turn. Welcome to Lunar Academy. Which House Will You Choose?

Gloria Mayor, better known as Glow, is on a deadline. If she can't tap into her magic soon, she'll be kicked out of Lunar Academy. Desperate times call for desperate measures, and in this case, that means accepting help from the talented and sexy Lionel.

Lionel Daniels is being punished for the actions of his father, a man he barely knows. When finds himself on magical probation, he chooses to focus his attention on helping Glow tap into hers. So what if he jumped on the opportunity because he wanted a way to get closer to her?

When the two find themselves trapped in a dire situation, they soon realize Glow tapping into her magic becomes less about flirting and more to do with survival, but that doesn't make the spark between them any less explosive.

Available Now